"Don't hide from me, Tru. I want you so badly, love," Thane murmured as he pulled her into his arms, cradling her there.

The world was spinning behind her closed eyelids as Tru felt Thane's mouth on her throat, the blood racing through her veins in a torrent of sensation. It was an ecstatic feeling, like nothing she'd ever known.

"Thane." Tru shuddered as she breathed his name. "I want you to love me, and I want to love you back."

His arms tightened around her, and he laughed huskily. "You've only to say the word, my love. I'm yours. . . ."

Bantam Books by Helen Mittermeyer

SURRENDER
  (*Loveswept #2*)

BRIEF DELIGHT
  (*Loveswept #15*)

UNEXPECTED SUNRISE
  (*Loveswept #57*)

VORTEX
  (*Loveswept #67*)

TEMPEST
  (*Loveswept #121*)

WHAT ARE *LOVESWEPT* ROMANCES?

They are stories of true romance and touching emotion. We believe those two very important ingredients are constants in our highly sensual and very believable stories in the *LOVESWEPT* line. Our goal is to give you, the reader, stories of consistently high quality that may sometimes make you laugh, sometimes make you cry, but are always fresh and creative and contain many delightful surprises within their pages.

Most romance fans read an enormous number of books. Those they truly love, they keep. Others may be traded with friends and soon forgotten. We hope that each *LOVESWEPT* romance will be a treasure—a "keeper." We will always try to publish

LOVE STORIES YOU'LL NEVER FORGET
BY AUTHORS YOU'LL ALWAYS REMEMBER

The Editors

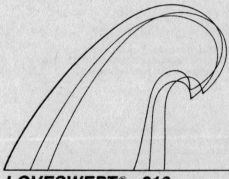

LOVESWEPT® • 210
Helen Mittermeyer
Kismet

 BANTAM BOOKS
TORONTO • NEW YORK • LONDON • SYDNEY • AUCKLAND

KISMET

A Bantam Book / October 1987

*LOVESWEPT® and the wave device are registered
trademarks of Bantam Books, Inc. Registered in U.S. Patent
and Trademark Office and elsewhere.*

*If you would be interested in receiving protective vinyl
covers for your Loveswept books, please write to this address
for information:*

> *Loveswept
> Bantam Books
> P.O. Box 985
> Hicksville, NY 11802*

ISBN 0-553-21773-9

Published simultaneously in the United States and Canada

---

*Bantam Books are published by Bantam Books, Inc. Its trade-
mark, consisting of the words "Bantam Books" and the por-
trayal of a rooster, is Registered in U.S. Patent and Trademark
Office and in other countries. Marca Registrada. Bantam
Books, Inc., 666 Fifth Avenue, New York, New York 10103.*

PRINTED IN THE UNITED STATES OF AMERICA

O   0 9 8 7 6 5 4 3 2 1

One

Leaning against his Ferrari, Thane Stoner studied the blonde who had just pulled her car into the parking space across from his. She patted her hair, glanced into the rearview mirror, and fidgeted with her earring. Ah, he thought, the woman was nervous.

She got out of the battered VW, slammed and locked the door, then stood staring at the ranch style house in front of her. Its windows and doors were open, and from them Tru could hear the sounds of a party in full swing, music and laughter blending in strident harmony.

But for some reason, she couldn't quite make herself march up the walkway and go in. She knew she needed a boost tonight. If she'd stayed home alone in her apartment, she would have gone crazy. Yet now that she'd reached Ellen's house, she wasn't sure she really felt like partying.

Earlier, on the way home from her class at UCLA she'd actually decided to call Ellen and tell her she couldn't come tonight. She was exhausted from cracking the books, working at a part-time job, and trying to keep what little was left of her personal life from shattering completely. She desperately needed an early night. But her promise to herself to get some rest had flown right out the window when she'd arrived home and found the divorce notice from Roger's lawyer. She'd showered in a fevered haste to get out of the apartment she'd shared with her husband and see other people who could distract her. She simply couldn't stand to contemplate her future.

Now, looking down at her left hand, she felt bile rise in her throat, misery well in her heart. She yanked the narrow gold band from her finger and put it in the pocket of her dress.

The blonde's abrupt gesture startled Thane. The elusively lovely woman seemed tensed like a bird poised for flight, and now he was positive that she didn't look forward to going to the party. As he surveyed her, he realized that her blond hair was lighter than he'd first thought. It was piled on top of her head where it caught and trapped the moonlight. The iridescence of her skin was straight out of fantasy, and the night breeze made the lightweight fabric of her dress cling to her tall, lissome body. His gaze traveled slowly over her frame once more. He'd certainly known more beautiful women, but never one who had tantalized him so much on first sight. His reaction both annoyed and titillated him.

He strolled over to her and asked softly, "Are you going in or are you parking cars?"

The rich, amused drawl of the masculine voice startled Tru. She looked hard at the tall man who stood in front of her, his face illuminated by the trapezoid of light coming from a window of the house. Handsome, self-assured, he caused a jolt of wariness to leap through her body. Something about this man made her want to escape him. Why? Her responses were odd . . . so foolish that she immediately clamped down on them.

"I'm not parking cars," she answered him at last, a lemony tartness in her voice that she hoped would put him off. On a night like this she certainly didn't need to risk an exchange with a large, insolent, unsettling stranger. She was glad for the shadowy anonymity of the night until she noted that he'd shifted position so that his back blocked the light coming from the house. She couldn't see his face at all now, but she could sense him inching closer to her. Her tongue flicked over her lips and her gaze touched him before moving to the house, then back again.

"Is something wrong?" Thane asked.

"Just having second thoughts about going in, I guess."

"I'm late too. Shall we arrive together?" He had an urgent desire to see her in full light. He held out his hand to her.

"All right," she replied. Why not? Hadn't she come here to forget her troubles, to bury Roger and memories of their disastrous marriage for at least a few short hours? The hot, reckless feeling that had made her dress quickly and push the speed limit while driving over took hold of her again. Why shouldn't she have fun? Soon enough she'd have to figure out how she was going to earn her own living . . . and face the fact that she would have to give up her pursuit of a degree in order to do so.

When she felt the stranger's hands on her upper arms, turning her so that the light from the house shone on her face, she looked up, startled. "What is it?" The quaver in her voice disconcerted her.

"I just wanted to see if I was imagining things. Thank heaven I wasn't. You're lovely and very fragile looking, even though you're tall." Thane inhaled the soft fragrance that seemed a part of her.

"Me, fragile? I'll have you know I was on my college swimming and tennis teams. Looks are deceiving. I'm not a bit delicate."

"When did you graduate?"

"I didn't. I'm back working for my degree." She didn't add that she would soon be dropping out. Why tell a stranger her life story?

"Let's join the party." Thane released his hold on her reluctantly but as they approached the door he reached again for her hand.

His touch gave Tru a strangely warm feeling. She was sure she had never seen him before and asked, "Are you a friend of Ellen's?"

"More a friend of her family's. My name is Thane Stoner. And you?"

"I'm Tru Hubbard. Ellen Sandilin and I went to school together."

Thane Stoner paused, his hand loosely clasping hers. "Oh? Are you one of the three musketeers Andy is always talking about?"

Thane Stoner? Maybe she *had* heard that name before. "What? Oh yes. Ellen and Maggie and I were always together. But Maggie is married and living in the East now."

"Are you married?"

"Just on the verge of being single again," Tru said more curtly than she'd meant to.

"I see."

"I thought you might." Tru preceded him through the door, stunned momentarily by the blast of party noises that hit her as she walked in. She felt unaccountably reassured by the hand that rose to her waist, steadying her.

"Tru! You *did* come. I'm so glad. I want you to meet Randy . . ." Ellen's exuberant hug and non-stop chatter made Tru feel happy in spite of herself. When Ellen looked over her friend's shoulder and caught sight of Thane, her smile widened. "Thane! I'm so glad you're here. I've been accusing that brother of mine all night of not inviting you. But Andy swore he had, and I'm glad he was telling the truth. A hunk like you is always a welcome addition to a party, you know." Ellen grinned impudently. Then her brow knitted. "I didn't know you two knew each other."

"We met outside. How are you, brat?" Thane leaned down and kissed Ellen's cheek. "Ah, I see your brother and Clare across the room. I'll just go over and say hi. Excuse me, Tru."

"Of course."

Ellen watched him for a few seconds, then pounced on her friend. "How did you manage to walk in with the biggest sex bomb in all of California—not to mention the richest." Ellen took her friend's arm and squeezed it. "I told you about him. He was Andy's roommate at the university. Remember the one I said played pro football for a while, then became a lawyer?" Ellen paused to take a breath and greet someone, before turning back to Tru. "He's sort of given up law now to concentrate on the family businesses. They're in orange juice, wineries, oil . . ."

"Sounds healthy."

"You can laugh if you want to, but Andy thinks Thane could be the next governor of our fair state. He's old money, Tru. And you know what they say— that's the best kind." Ellen edged her friend through the hordes of people, introducing her to everyone she could; she didn't pause until they reached the small bar that had been set up in a corner of her living room.

Once there Ellen warmly clasped Tru's hand.

"What's wrong? You're absolutely chalky. And I had the strongest feeling that you wouldn't show up tonight."

"I wasn't going to—until I read my mail."

Ellen looked puzzled for a moment, then her eyes widened. "You don't mean that Roger actually went through with it?"

"I got my first divorce papers today." Dry-eyed, but shaky, Tru stared at her friend. "I suppose I should have expected it. He called me this morning to say that he had decided we needed to be apart longer to settle our problems." She inhaled sharply. "He also said that he was letting the lease on the apartment go."

"The low life! After you struggled so, working two jobs in order for him to get his master's and start on his thesis. Dammit, I told you at the time you shouldn't have given up your own schooling to help him." Ellen squeezed harder on Tru's hand. "Get a lawyer and sue him. Make him pay for *your* education. He owes you that much." Ellen hugged her friend. "What will you do, Tru?"

"I've been trying not to dwell on it. In fact, I was hoping this party would help me relax and forget it all for a while. Do you have any magic potion that can do that? Because I've decided to table all tough decisions and have a wild time tonight."

Ellen hugged her again and grinned. "Since all you drink is juice that should be something to see."

"I'll drink something with additives. How about a monosodium glutamate cocktail?" Tru was feeling giddy all of a sudden.

The two friends laughed together, then turned toward the bar to order.

"One wild orange juice, on the rocks, and a beer for me," Ellen ordered.

In a few minutes Ellen was called away by hostess

duties, and just as she moved into the crowd, Tru cast about for someone she knew to talk to.

"Hi. Would you like to dance?" Tru heard the deep voice ask from behind her.

She was about to say no, when she stopped herself. She wasn't likely to have a good time standing in a corner all night. "Sure," she said.

Much to her surprise, she did begin to enjoy herself.

"My name is Gil," her partner told her during a break between songs. "You really know how to move," he added admiringly.

Tru just smiled and let her body respond to the music.

When they paused to sip their drinks, Gil gestured to another man. "This is my friend, George. I can tell he wants to cut in."

So Tru danced with Gil's friend.

When they stopped she was out of breath and laughing and facing another man who smiled at her.

"Hi. My name's Randy. I'm Ellen's date. She's told me all about you." Tru looked taken aback for an instant, but then Randy grinned. "Don't worry. Everything she said was good. Want to dance?"

Tru laughed out loud, liking Ellen's lanky companion immediately.

"I can't believe it. You look as much like a teenager as Ellen does. Was something in the water at that school you both attended?"

"You should see Maggie. She makes both of us look like old women. Well, she's pregnant at the moment, but ordinarily she looks like Peter Pan."

"Lord, that's awful." Out of the corner of his eye Randy glanced at Ellen, who was smiling and talking ebulliently in the middle of a group of merrymakers across the room. "I'm afraid if I take her home to my parents they'll think she's sixteen, not twenty-five. My father will take a horsewhip to me."

Tru was glad to see how much this smiling young man seemed to care for Ellen, and decided to make a leading statement. "Sounds like you're serious about Ellen."

"I am. I hope I can convince her of it, though."

"If you're the Randy that she's always talking about, it shouldn't be too difficult." Tru chuckled, feeling more relaxed than she had in a long time as Randy spun her, making her dress billow out around her legs.

"Thanks, Tru. I'm glad we finally had a chance to meet. Ellen wanted you to come to this party. She says you work too hard." He kissed her cheek when the music ended and, as Tru could see he wanted to be with Ellen, she excused herself.

She found the orange juice she'd put down when she'd begun to dance, gratefully sipped it, then wandered over to greet Clare and Andy, Ellen's brother and sister-in-law. They talked for a few minutes. When others came up to speak to them, Tru moved away.

"You're the toast of the party. But you must be thirsty after all that dancing. Let me get you a refill." Thane steered her toward the bar again.

"Thank you, Mr. Stoner. Orange juice, please." She smiled at him, silently blessing the anesthetizing effect the music and crowd were having on her.

"Please call me Thane." He handed her a drink, then sipped his own whiskey and water, studying her flushed cheeks. She had eyes like sapphires and he loved the pearly pinkness of her skin, her small-boned but tall, lithe build, the soft oval of her face. "When you've quenched your thirst, perhaps you'd like to dance again."

"I would, thank you." Tru was surprised to find

him at her side. Every time she'd looked his way before this, there had been a cluster of women around him. It amused her that some of the women who'd been at Stoner's side were now glowering at her. Heavens, what did the man have? The magnetism of Apollo?

Tru shook herself free of her skepticism. What did it matter if he was a stud? This was her night for forgetting and having fun.

In her heart of hearts, though, Tru knew she couldn't make up for all the good times she'd missed in the last five years. From the day she and Roger had married, her life had been one hurdle after another, one more chore to tackle, another responsibility to add to the list. They had been building a life together, or so she thought, which was the reason she had worked so hard to put Roger through school. He'd only landed his first full-time job six months ago. Shortly after that he'd told her that he was leaving. He had problems to sort out. Since then he'd sent her barely enough money to continue her studies, pay the bills, and cover the rent.

"Hey, come out of the dream." Thane sounded irritated. He wasn't used to having a female companion stare down into her drink, her mind obviously far away from him.

"Oh. Sorry." Tru looked up at him and was jolted out of her reverie. Thane Stoner's eyes were the color of good Kentucky bourbon. They were glinting over her now, giving her goose bumps. Suddenly, though, her husband's face intruded again. Roger! If only she could stop thinking of him.

Thane caught the flash of hurt and bewilderment in her eyes and reached, without thinking, to catch her close to him.

Blood thumped through him at the contact with her slender form. It rocked him. He couldn't believe how much she excited him. Whoa! he told himself. Take it easy. She's vulnerable right now, in the throes of a divorce.

The beat of the love song that came from the stereo swelled in Tru's blood. She closed her eyes and leaned against Thane, loving it when his arm tightened around her.

Without speaking they began to move to the music.

"What does the Tru stand for?" she heard him breathe into her ear.

"Gertrude."

Thane tilted his head and smiled down at her. "I've never known a girl named Gertrude."

"Lucky you." She smiled up at him. "My parents were English teachers with a fondness for Shakespeare. They named me after Hamlet's mother."

They smiled broadly at one another then, and an electric silence settled over them. At last, Thane released her hand and let his arms drift down to her waist, then around to the small of her back. It seemed completely natural to Tru to entwine her arms around his neck.

They danced to a medley of melodies, their bodies close.

The music stopped for a moment while someone changed records, but they didn't separate.

Tru didn't know how long they danced on like that, as if in a magic circle. It was only when Ellen called them to come and eat that they moved apart.

"Shall we get some food?" Thane asked her lazily.

She nodded, glancing up at him, feeling a flush rise to her cheeks. Did he think she was a fool, hanging on to him the way she had? What was wrong with her? "I've monopolized you long enough, Mr. Stoner . . . Thane . . ."

"I'm not complaining." He touched her nose with one finger. "Let's eat."

"All right." Tru felt a surge of relief that he wasn't leaving her. Then she could have booted herself in the backside, because she was attaching too much significance to her encounter with this man . . . a man she couldn't afford to see after tonight. She had problems to settle, a new life to work out. She didn't dare complicate things further by bringing Thane Stoner into the picture.

Nevertheless, Tru couldn't help but feel happy with him as she followed him to the buffet, let him fill her plate with food, and then joined him at an empty table on the patio.

"Good food," she mumbled, feeling awkward and embarrassed with Thane now. She'd plastered her body to him while they'd danced . . . and danced. Lord, how long had they been out on the floor? Blood suffused her face at the thought.

"In a cloud again?" Thane asked gently. He found her bewitching. Just as he drew one conclusion about her, she seemed to change and present an entirely different picture to him. Tru Hubbard was an emotional chameleon, he decided, but an adorable one. He watched the flush rise in the smooth skin of her graceful neck and wished that he were the one she'd been dwelling on for such long periods during the evening. "Let me take you to dinner tomorrow evening,'" he said suddenly.

Startled, Tru's gaze flew to his face. "I can't do that. I'm married."

"Just on the verge of being single again is the way I think you described it. Right?"

For some reason her own words stung. All at once she felt raw and cold. "I did say that, I guess."

"Then how about dinner?"

"I don't think . . ." her words trailed off as she envisioned the lonely nights ahead, anticipating how awful she'd feel when she told Professor Blazow that she'd be dropping out of his Greek Drama class and abandoning her goal of a degree in English literature, at least for the foreseeable future. The older man with the vandyke beard had been her mentor and friend since she'd started back at the university and Tru was fond of him. Damn! There was so much to face, so much confusion in her life.

Thane almost bent his supper fork out of shape waiting for her to answer. She had gone into one of her reveries again. Who was she thinking about? Who had such control over her? "You were saying?" he asked loudly.

"What?" Tru blinked at him. At the moment he seemed to her like a lifeline. She grabbed hold. "I would love to join you for dinner, Mr. Stoner."

"Thane, please." He chuckled, relieved that she'd accepted, yet annoyed with the effect he allowed her to have on him. What a damned pubescent fool he was to get in a sweat about a female he'd only met a few hours ago! It amazed him that, at that moment, he couldn't recall the face of the woman with whom he'd been having a heavy relationship for the last two months.

"Thane." Tru smiled back at him, feeling that hot recklessness again. "I hope you'll take me someplace where the food is good. I have a huge appetite."

"Really?" Thane glanced at the barely touched food on her plate, seeing the desperation behind her cocky grin. "Don't worry, lady. I'll make sure you get enough to eat."

"Good." Tru pushed some of the rolled ham around on her plate. "You were Andy's roommate at the university, right?"

"Yes." He could see she was fighting the pull of cloudy thoughts again. "Would you like to go out to the park one day and play football with me?" The words had rolled out of his mouth before he'd had a chance to think them through.

Tru's head flew up and she stared at him open-mouthed, her fork poised in the air above her plate. "You don't mean it. You played pro ball! Why would you want to play sandlot with an amateur?"

"Are you an amateur football player?"

"Well, maybe not exactly that. The three of us, Ellen, Maggie and I, used to make Andy play and we would all jump on him." Tru laughed. "You should have seen him one Thanksgiving morning when we played. We shoved him into the mud and sat on him."

Thane felt elated by her mirth. She was lovely when she laughed and the thought that he had helped to evoke it made him happier still.

Ellen came over to them with Randy in tow. "Everyone is mad at the two of you. You've been so exclusive."

"Just having a good time at your party, brat," Thane told her good-humoredly, noticing Tru's flush.

Randy rolled his eyes. "I tried to talk her out of coming over here. But you know Ellen . . ."

"Now you've made Tru blush, Randy." Ellen patted her friend's hand.

Andy then joined the group, commenting to Ellen, "If I know you, kid, you're probably the one who made Tru blush." Andy grinned wickedly when Tru glared at him. "Do I embarrass you, too, other sister?"

"Turn blue, Alex." Tru laughed with the rest of them, but she wanted to melt into the woodwork.

"She's been telling stories about you, Andy, about the time the three musketeers pushed you into the mud during a football game."

"More than once." Andy grimaced. "They were terrible."

In minutes Ellen was rattling off one anecdote after another about her brother.

Tru breathed a sigh of relief that the focus was off her, her smile touching Thane who kept on watching her all the time Ellen spoke.

During a lull in the lively conversation, Tru glanced at her watch and smothered a groan. It was late and she'd have to get up early. "It's been a wonderful party, Ellen, but I have to go." Tru rose to her feet. "But first I'll help you straighten up."

Randy held up his hand, palm outward. "No. Ellen insists I do that." He turned his hands over. "But if she makes me do dishes and I get dishpan hands, I'll sue."

There were guffaws from all around.

Tru noticed that Thane was standing. She turned to him. "Thank you. It was fun dancing with you." Putting her hand out to him, she shook his once, then made quick good-byes to the others.

She had almost reached her car when she felt a hand on her arm. Startled she turned to face Thane. "What is it, Thane?"

"I need to know your address to pick you up for dinner tomorrow night."

"Oh. It might be better if I could meet you somewhere."

Thane shrugged. "If you prefer."

"I do."

"Then let's make it the Thayer at seven."

"Fine." She didn't look at him again as she unlocked her car door and got behind the wheel. Thanks to all the Graces, her old VW started on the first try and didn't stall once as she drove away.

If flashed through her mind on the way home that she really didn't have an outfit dressy enough for the Thayer. She'd have to wear the one she had on. "That'll teach him. He'll never ask me out again. On the other hand, maybe he won't notice if I wear the same dress two nights in a row." Tru knew there wasn't the chance of an ice cube in Hades that that would be so. Thane Stoner was a very observant man.

She was reeling with exhaustion by the time she parked her car outside her building and went up the elevator to the fourth floor. Even so, sleep was a long time coming. Visions of Thane Stoner marched through her mind. In a way it was a relief to think of him. It kept her mind off Roger and the blankness of her future.

Two

The next day was just as bad as Tru had feared it might be. All of her instructors tried to persuade her not to quit, Professor Blazow trying the hardest.

"My dear, you've taken hold here. You have an academic future. I insist that you reevaluate your position."

Eyes stinging, Tru shook her head. "I can't right now, Professor Blazow. Perhaps sometime . . ." Her voice trailed away, her eyes avoiding his face.

"You're hurting, Gertrude. Can I help you?"

"Thank you, no, Professor." Tru clutched the hand he held out to her. "But I want you to know that your friendship has meant a great deal to me."

They shook hands, and Tru promised that she'd make coming back to school her highest priority.

That afternoon she visited an employment office, then made the rounds of some of the companies on a list she'd been given. Filling out forms and having interviews was tedious, especially as she got nowhere. Everyone was polite, but all said the same thing: Tru was either under- or overqualified for every position.

At the end of the day she walked into her apartment like a zombie, too tired to face an evening with Thane Stoner. She went right to the phone book, thumbing through it. Thane Stoner wasn't listed! What was the name of his company? His law office? What businesses did Ellen say he was in?

The phone rang at her elbow, startling her. "Yes?"

"Tru? Roger. I suppose you have the papers?"

"Yes."

"Good. My lawyer wants to meet with you as soon as possible. Is Monday all right?"

"Monday? Well, I don't know, Roger. I don't have a lawyer yet."

"You don't need one. All you have to do is listen to what my lawyer has to say and sign some things."

"I think I should have a lawyer under the circumstances."

Roger sighed heavily. "Tru, don't make trouble. It won't change things."

"I'm not the one who's making trouble. I'll get back to you." She hung up the phone and put a shaking hand to her mouth just as the doorbell rang. She opened it a crack.

"Flowers for Gertrude Hubbard." When Tru undid the chain, the messenger handed her a bouquet of roses, along with a small corsage in a box. "Tip's already taken care of, ma'am," the young man said and grinned at her.

"Thank you." Tru stared at the masses of creamy roses, glistening with moisture, nestling among the lush green of ferns. She barely noticed how long she stood there, or that her tears had dampened the flowers even more.

She buried her face in the flowers. They made her feel feminine, her skin softer, more luminescent, her body supple and relaxed. Gradually her gloominess dissipated, and she became her old fiery self.

Tru Hubbard was no doormat and Roger wasn't going to walk all over her!

The card fell to the floor when she laid the roses on the sink and put the corsage into the refrigerator. Tru bent down to retrieve it, her hand trembling slightly as she opened the little envelope and read:

"TO THE BEAUTIFUL LADY WHO DREW ME TO THE PARTY LAST NIGHT. DO YOU BELIEVE IN KISMET? IN THE INEVITABLE MEETING? I DO, NOW."

There was no signature, but Tru didn't need one.

She arranged the blooms in a cut glass vase that Ellen had given her and set them on the coffee table.

She rushed into the shower, shampooing then blow-drying her long thick blond hair before doing her nails with pale peach polish. She wished for a moment she had something else to wear besides the deep peach-colored dress she'd worn last night, then put the thought out of her mind.

She caught her hair up in a roll on the crown of her head, wispy strands curtaining her face.

She wore no earrings or jewelry other than the thin gold watch her parents had given her for her high school graduation. Suddenly she missed them with a pain that left her breathless. They had died in the sky-jacking of a plane when they'd been on a vacation in Greece five years before. It had taken Tru a long time to put the tragedy behind her. Even now, hardly a day went by when she didn't think of them.

She retrieved from a drawer the old-fashioned beaded purse that she'd bought in a thrift shop, then slipped on the sleek gold high heels that had stayed in a box at the bottom of the closet since her marriage to Roger. He was the same height as she and didn't like her to appear taller. Last night, out of habit, she had worn her patent leather flats.

As she left the apartment she was assailed by

melancholy, but she touched the corsage she'd affixed to her wrist and lifted her chin, putting all her worries on hold and trying to concentrate on the evening ahead.

More than once during the trip to the downtown hotel, she had the urge to turn around and go home. More than once horns blared as other drivers swung around her and Tru realized that she'd drifted near the other lane.

When she finally arrived at the Thayer, she pulled into the circular driveway leading up to the front door, grimacing when she saw the valet parking sign and realized that she couldn't back out because there was a Rolls Royce brougham behind her.

Tru smiled at the valet, who blinked at her rusted VW with its bashed-in passenger door, and then smiled back, helping her out as perfectly politely as if she were the lady in the Rolls.

Lifting her chin she marched under the marquee leading to the gold scrolled door, hoping that the look she gave the doorman as she passed him didn't telegraph the quaking of her insides. What was she doing here?

"Good evening," Thane said, appearing at her side. "You wore the flowers. Thank you." He leaned down and kissed her cheek even before a startled Tru could do more than say "Hello."

"Shall we go up?"

"Up?" Tru followed his gaze to the glassed-in elevator before them. "Heavens." Her calves suddenly felt as if they were turning to jelly. She had never liked heights.

"All set?"

"Oh yes," she said bravely.

Thane felt her body quiver when they entered the elevator and it started to rise. He slipped his arm around her waist and pulled her close to him. "Would you rather not look down?"

"Actually I'd love to. I just don't know if I can."

"Well, I'll hold you. That might help." Thane could feel his blood slam through his veins as he enfolded her close to him, pressing her back against his body, one arm at her waist, the other across her chest, her breasts thrusting against his arm. "Is that better?" he asked her huskily.

"Yes." Tru felt dizzy, but she knew it wasn't from the height. The strong body at her back made her whole being vibrate with a need that she had never before experienced. Safe in his powerful arms Tru let herself look around as the elevator rose rapidly; before long the people in the lobby below seemed like ants. "It's wonderful. We're so high," she breathed delightedly.

Thane felt as if they might go right on through the roof as he leaned his chin on her hair and tightened his hold. The softness of her silk-clad body was enough to make him dizzy. She had such small bones, yet her body was large and firm and strong.

When the elevator glided to a stop and the doors opened behind them, they both sighed and moved apart.

The Penthouse Gold room was filled to capacity. A number of patrons waited to be seated, and a large group stood talking at the bar. Others were dancing on the parquet floor in the supper club adjacent to the restaurant.

"I thought you might like to eat in the dining room and listen to the string quartet. Then, if you want, we could move to the club for dancing."

Tru felt shaken to her core. How long had it been since she'd felt cherished? Cared for? Pampered?

She looked up at her escort. "I can't stay out too late tonight. I have lots to do tomorrow."

"Like what?" Thane asked, though he didn't want her thinking about anything but the present, or of anyone else but him.

Tru could hear the tremulousness in her voice as she at last began to speak. "For one thing I have to get a lawyer. My husband wants me to meet with him and his lawyer next week and I have a feeling I should be represented."

"You're right there." Thane waved away the attendant who was about to hold Tru's chair and seated her himself. "Bring me a phone please," he told the hovering man.

In minutes the phone appeared and Thane was dialing. "David. How are you? Yes. I want you to do something for me. I have a friend who needs a lawyer and I know you've been looking for clients. Yes, you heard me right. I'm sure you'll charge an equitable fee." There was a long pause. "How astute you are. I was certain you would understand me. She'll call at your office in the morning. Her name is Tru Hubbard. Say, about ten? Good. Thanks." Thane hung up the phone, waving for the waiter to carry it away. "There. One of your concerns is taken care of."

"But—" Tru began, but immediately stopped herself from protesting vehemently. As much as she appreciated what he'd done, she couldn't let herself be railroaded by this forceful man. "I have some questions . . ."

"Shoot."

"Are you *sure* he's good? I mean, I may not have enough money for one of the best lawyers in town, but it would be foolish of me not to get the best one I can." Her voice trailed off as she noticed Thane's mouth harden and his chin jut forward. "You think I'm being ungrateful, don't you?" she asked quickly.

"David's very good. And I assure you he's very reasonable."

"Is he a friend of yours?"

"I've been dealing with him for years."

"Look, I'm sorry, but I just haven't known you long enough for that to be an endorsement."

Thane couldn't believe it. No one, especially no woman, had ever questioned him in such a fashion. "I thought I was doing you a favor."

"And so you are, but you must understand my situation. I have to be able to have total confidence in whomever I hire, because I'm in danger of losing everything I own. My husband is pulling the rug out from under me." Tru sighed, putting her chin in her hands. "I wasn't going to talk about this tonight. Why did I bring it up?"

"I don't know." Anger and amusement warred within Thane as he stared at the woebegone child-woman facing him.

Tru sighed. "Now you're getting testy."

"At this moment I could paddle your bottom right in the middle of that dance floor. Is that being testy?"

A bubble of laughter burst from her. Oddly enough Thane Stoner's unstifled anger pleased her. It was a hundred percent better than the injured, silent treatment Roger had given her whenever they'd disagreed. "You wouldn't dare, Stoner."

"I'll probably have to someday. Because you'll probably deserve it!" he told her silkily before a reluctant smile touched his mouth. He almost lifted her from her chair when he leaned over and cupped her chin in his palms. His kiss was bruising and exciting.

"Spoilsport," Tru told him, out of breath, when he lifted his head.

"How can you say that? I'll take you on anytime."

He decided that sparring with her was going to be one of their most delightful activities. "And, incidentally, David Wilson is an excellent lawyer. You can call the Bar Association and ask them if you like." Thane hadn't moved away from her, and his heart was pounding with excitement as her breath mingled with his.

Tru sat back, knowing there were other things she should find out about David Wilson, but at the moment she couldn't quite seem to work up a sense of urgency about anything other than the feel of Thane's lips on hers.

The gypsy music coming from the string quartet seemed to be guiding the blood through her veins. Part of her was stunned by the way she'd warmed to Thane Stoner. Tru had become very leery of people since the break-up of her marriage. Was she really ready now to put her faith in a man she'd known for just twenty-four hours? "Now all I need to do is find an inexpensive apartment and I'll be in business," she continued. "Please don't tell me you're in real estate. I won't believe it."

"All right. I won't tell you that." He smiled back, leaning even closer, kissing her on the nose. It delighted him when she didn't pull back. "What's wrong with where you're living now?"

"Roger isn't picking up the rent and I can't afford it on what I'll be able to earn . . . if I manage to land a job."

"I could get you a job in one of our companies."

Tru shook her head. "I don't think I should let you do that. You've done enough for me by getting me a respectable lawyer."

"Let me rephrase that. I'll check around. If there's a spot you can fill, I'll let you know."

"You won't create a job just for me?"

"No. If there isn't an opening, I'll tell you."

Tru bit her lip. "That's very kind of you, but—"

"No strings attached. I'll even put it in writing for you if you like." He chuckled.

Tears rose in her eyes like oil in a Texas gusher. Her body shook with the depth of her feeling. "Sorry. I don't know what's the matter with me."

Thane hitched his chair around so that his broad shoulders shielded her from view of the people in the dining room. Taking a linen handkerchief from his pocket, he dabbed at the corners of her eyes. "It's all right to cry. I think you need it," he told her calmly as she fought to control herself. "It's all right, Tru. It really is."

For long moments she only nodded, swallowing over and over, the shudders slowly subsiding. "Thank you."

"You've been on the razor's edge, darling." Thane looked around and the waiter appeared, as if he had been conjured. Then he ordered for both of them.

By the time the food arrived, Tru was more in control of herself. She finished her soup at Thane's urging, then ate broiled prawns that were so delicately and perfectly spiced, she didn't leave one on her plate. Neither of them ordered dessert; instead they nibbled on cheese and fruit. Tru felt replete but not uncomfortable, once again on an even keel.

"I think you should have a little of this." Thane cajoled her into sipping some of his Napoleon brandy.

Tru coughed at the first sip, but then a warming sensation traveled all the way down to her knees. She had to admit it felt delicious.

"Now I think we should dance."

Tru stared at him. She didn't want him to prolong their date if he didn't really want to, especially after she'd made such a scene. "I am sorry for breaking down like that and I'll understand if you'd like to leave." She shot a look toward the club. "Besides, it's very crowded in there."

"Let me worry about that." Thane helped her from her chair, taking her arm and threading his way through the tables to the other room where the dance band had drawn people like a magnet.

Tru noticed the infinitesimal tilt of Thane's head when he caught the eye of the maître d'. A reserved card was whisked off a table situated in sight of the bandstand, yet secluded by a semicircle of tall plants. "You must own the place to be able to do that."

"Yes." Thane grinned down at her. She shot him a startled look.

She only had time to place her purse on the table before he led her to the dance floor and pulled her into his arms. "I think you must be some sort of magician."

"Not true. I asked you once if you believed in Kismet. Remember? Our meeting was inevitable, and I figured you would agree with me. I'm just making sure that nothing gets in the way of our destiny."

Tru looked up into his smiling face, seeing the steely glint in those bourbon-colored eyes.

A frisson of delight ran up her spine.

Three

When Tru saw David Wilson's office with its battalion of secretaries and office staff in the glass and steel high-rise, her heart plummeted.

"How do you do, Mrs. Hubbard? I'm David Wilson. Let's get right to it, shall we?"

"Mr. Wilson, I don't think I should be here," she began. She tried to smile, but the result was dismal.

David studied her for a moment, then pushed a sheet of paper toward her. "This is our agreement, Mrs. Hubbard. All my fees and what I intend to do for you are on it. Sit down, won't you? Read it and tell me what you think."

Dazed, Tru stared at the small fee before sinking into a chair in front of the mammoth teak desk. "I . . . I think it's fine."

An hour and a half later she left the office buoyed by hope. Though David had argued with her when she told him she wanted nothing from Roger, there had been an affinity between them that gave her a measure of self-confidence about the days and months ahead. All she wanted from the divorce were her family mementos. He understood that. Tru had found David to be patient and prudent, but still convinced that they could fight back and win.

Tru made the rounds of the employment offices after that and found nothing.

Thane called her when she returned home and told her that he had a job for her as a receptionist at the Pillor Building and that she would be able to apply for student aid if she decided to continue with her education.

"Thane," she said thickly, knowing she should tell him that she couldn't take it, that it was better to be independent than obligated to someone. Still, it was a job, and a good one, at that.

"Don't say anything. Just be ready. I'm picking you up in an hour."

For the next two weeks Tru saw Thane every moment that she wasn't studying, or at class, or working at the Pillor Building. He was becoming the focus in her life and not even Greek Drama and Professor Blazow—who'd been overjoyed when she came back—could blunt the hurricane force of his personality.

It had taken her a few days to get used to the telephone system in the Pillor Building, but once she did she found the job fun, and since it didn't entail anything other than answering calls and taking messages, she was able to use her spare time to study.

She saw Roger a few times at their lawyers' offices, once when he came to get the computer he'd left behind, and another time when he arrived to complain about the amount of money she would be getting in the divorce settlement.

"I don't see why you need a lump sum, Tru," he'd told her petulantly.

"Because you will not be making monthly payments to me. And my lawyer thought that since I put you through school, you owed it to me. Frankly, Roger, I think he has a point."

Then, when he discovered that she had found a smaller apartment closer to the university, he'd acted upset. "Why does that bother you?" she'd asked. "I have only a week left on this lease. Should I have gotten a park bench?"

"Don't be cute, Tru. It doesn't become you. Why didn't you get a penthouse? I wouldn't expect less after the expensive lawyer you hired."

He hadn't always been so mean, so vitriolic, she thought. He seemed a stranger to her now. She wondered whether the bitter change in him had to do with his disappointment over not landing a job in the academic world. He'd gotten something in private industry, but to him that was second best— never an easy position for Roger Hubbard to accept.

"My lawyer and his prestige or lack of it are none of your business," she had said. "You didn't get the bill, did you?" Tru felt hot all over as she recalled the reverent way Roger's lawyer had treated David Wilson when the four of them had met to discuss the terms of the divorce. That night when she'd questioned Thane he'd been offhand about it. "I told you from the beginning that David was good, and you thought you could afford him, right? So? There's no problem."

It was awfully easy to get along with that. Besides when Thane kissed her good night, she forgot everything but the feel and taste of him.

Increasingly their good-byes were fraught with a passion that shook Tru to her very core. It shocked her to realize that in her whole married life with Roger, she'd never experienced feelings like those she did with Thane.

Two days before she was scheduled to move, she returned from work to find most of the furniture gone, including precious things that had belonged to her family. She tried to call Roger, but got no answer.

That evening when Thane arrived, he surveyed the wreckage, then the shattered expression on her face, and went directly to the phone. But Tru, sitting on a kitchen chair in the midst of the emptiness, looking around blankly, barely heard his harsh words and didn't even wonder who he was talking to.

"Did he take anything that you especially prize?"

"All the things that had belonged to my mother and father and my grandparents."

"Describe them," Thane ordered tersely, pulling a notebook with a gold pencil attached to it from his pocket, urging her on when she faltered.

He made another call, then looked back at her before hanging up. He knelt in front of her chair. "I'm going to call for take-out food tonight. While we're waiting for it, you and I are going to go over this list again to make sure you didn't forget anything. You're not to worry. I have someone who will handle this properly."

"Roger won't give up anything, I know."

"Put him out of your mind."

Tru moved to the smaller apartment in a house near the university. All the things that were on her list were in the apartment when she arrived.

"How did you manage it, Thane?" she asked, half concerned, half overjoyed at the return of the precious items.

But all she could get Thane to say was, "I have my ways." He said it smiling at her gently, cupping her chin in his hand. It made Tru feel like melting. She looked around and then sighed contentedly. Her grandmother's dishes were on a shelf above the faded sofa she'd found at Goodwill. "It wouldn't have been home without Grandmother's china and the paintings. My grandfather did those."

"Wouldn't you have liked a better bed?" Thane stuck his head in the bedroom, looking over his shoulder at Tru. "That's just box springs, a mattress and frame."

"It was on sale and it's very comfortable."

"Is it? I'll have to try it sometime," he said impudently.

Tru felt an overwhelming desire to tell him to try the bed any time he wished. "Take my word for it." Her voice had a croaky sound that, she was sure, he must have noticed.

He turned and strolled toward her, catching her nervously threading and unthreading her fingers. Leaning down, he kissed her nose. "I would never force you and I'm completely sincere about it, but that doesn't mean I won't try and convince you we should make love."

"That could hurt my divorce case." Tru gasped when he enfolded her in his arms. She felt like hot lava sliding down a mountain.

"We would be most discreet." Thane cuddled her close to him, his chin resting on her hair, the fragility and strength of her making the blood boil through his veins. He didn't feel like fighting his need to hold and caress her anymore. From the moment they met Tru Hubbard had given him an unbridled joy that both astounded and seared him. Getting entangled with a woman wasn't at all what he had in mind. Oh, he'd come close to marrying a time or two, but he had always escaped before the net fell. Rather for him the sophisticated affair where both parties understood the rules. But Thane was very sure that Tru didn't play by those rules.

Tru put both hands on his chest trying to create enough space between them so that she could look up at him. "We've seen each other every night for a month."

"So we have. If you're keeping track, don't forget the lunches in the park near the Pillor Building, and the breakfasts at the Acropolis Diner."

Tru nodded. "I love those Greek omelets." She pressed her lips together. How easily Thane could deter her! "Never mind."

"Don't say that. I like the omelets too."

"Thane, be serious. David told me that Roger's lawyer might try to make something tawdry out of our relationship. And that could give Roger leverage in the divorce case."

"Roger Hubbard is angry because you are in possession of what is rightfully yours. I don't need David to describe the kind of man Roger is." Thane tightened his hold on her. His jaw was clenched, the look in his eyes cold and stern. "He will not be allowed to cause you pain, I promise you that."

Tru lowered her head. "A scandal wouldn't be good for either of us, Thane. You're an important man. The tabloids would have a field day with anything Roger gave them. We have to take that into consideration."

"This is not the Victorian Age, darling. A man and a woman being together doesn't constitute front page news any more." He put his index finger on her lips when she opened her mouth to contradict him, shaking his head. "I've talked to David." Thane was brusque, his features taking on the rigid strength of newly cast iron. "I don't accept that we have to be separated. In fact, I fully intend to convince you to come and live with me. Together we'll handle any problems that arise." He was going to say more but then he clamped his lips together.

Tru stared up at him. "You know about Roger seeing a woman in his office, don't you? I mean, you seem to know everything."

Thane didn't answer her at first, just gave her a lingering kiss. "I hope that fool Roger didn't tell you about her."

Tru returned his kiss, leaning back to sigh deeply. "Andy was at Mercury Computers, where Roger works, one afternoon and saw him with her in the cafeteria. He told Ellen about it."

Thane pushed her hair off her forehead. "That must have hurt you."

"It would have a month ago," she admitted, leaning on him for a moment, recalling how unsurprised she was when Ellen had told her. "I think if I'd questioned his leaving me more deeply, I would have come up with that answer. There had to be another woman involved somehow, I guess." She shrugged. "A month ago I couldn't have been this objective about Roger. Now I just feel relieved that he is out of my life."

"Really?" Thane bent closer, his lips almost touching hers.

"Yes." His kiss mesmerized her, touching and teasing. Her eyes closed as though the lids were weighted.

When she felt the pressure of his mouth increasing on hers, she tilted her head slightly to give him easier access. The wonderful, sweet pulling sensation of his lips seemed to draw the very soul from her body.

Thane's blood thundered in his ears as his tongue traced the hot, sweet cavity of her mouth. He felt his body harden in response to the explosive sensuousness she was evoking in him. He wanted to bury himself in her, let her body manacle him to her; he'd willingly stay there for a lifetime.

With his mouth clamped to hers, he bent and placed a hand behind her knees, scooping her up into his arms. He moved his head a fraction, watching his eyelids lift. "Darling?"

Tru curled her hands around his shoulders, pressing her face into his neck, her lips fevered at touching the smooth surface of his skin. "I want you to love me, Thane," she said. Then regret cut through her like a knife. "But I can't let you until I know more of what's going on with the divorce."

Thane let her slide down his body, steadying her as she stood.

"Are you going to leave?" Tru felt painfully out of breath. Suddenly she recognized how patient he'd been with her for the past weeks.

If she'd been fair with him, she would have put him out of her troubled life weeks ago because of how rapidly they had become deeply involved with each other. But she hadn't had the strength to tell him to stay away. He had become too important to her too fast. Tru saw his face in the books she studied. Male mannequins in store windows took on his features. At night she fantasized that he was beside her, and often she'd woken hugging a pillow to her chest.

He blinked, looking down at her, seeing her distress, trying to tamp down the torrent of passion that had hardened his body and now made it throb with discomfort. "No. I'm not leaving but you may have to fill your bathtub with ice cubes and spend some time there." He chuckled as her face turned a bright pink. "How far does your blush go?"

"Far enough. I hope someday you'll see for yourself."

"Darling! My imagination exploded when it reached your navel."

"Thane!" Blood filled her face from both passion and embarrassment. His mind and emotions were so open to her. In all the time she'd spent with Roger she'd never felt she'd known him as well as she knew this man. She scrutinized his features. "It isn't because I don't want you to make love to me. I do. Nothing could make me happier than to have you take me in there, remove my clothes and—"

"No," Thane snapped. "Don't say any more. I don't think I can take it. Visions of you are rioting through my mind. My body is on fire." He stepped back, his face contorted.

"Would it help you to know that I feel the same frustration?" she asked.

"A little." His smile touched her sweetly. "It's just that sex never felt like purgatory before."

She swallowed hard, then said, as casually as she could, "And you've had *lots* of experience with it, no doubt."

"No doubt." He took up her challenge. Why hide his checkered past?

For a minute they faced off, glaring at each other like enemies, not lovers.

Tru gave in first. It all seemed so meaningless anyway. Who cares how many women he'd known before her? "Why did I say that to you?" she asked, her hands outstretched in apology.

"It wasn't your fault, it was mine. What the hell is the matter with me, barking at you like that?" Thane pulled her back into his arms, his head pressed to her hair. "Forgive me, Tru darling. You've been going through enough as it is."

"You have saved my life, Thane Stoner. Because of you there are no black days. I've never been better than when I'm with you." She embraced him. "Without you I would have gone mad these past weeks."

He pushed her away to look deep into her eyes.

His soulful gaze spoke volumes. Then, suddenly, he chuckled. "Would you like to see a movie tonight?"

She grinned. "I guess we shouldn't stay here."

"No," he replied simply.

"Could I have popcorn?"

"The minute we get there."

They spent two happy hours in the darkness of the theater, but all Tru saw on the screen was Thane's face. He was the hero, his gorgeous face framed perfectly. She was glad she didn't have to critique the movie afterwards. What would she have said? No one else had seen the picture starring Thane Stoner that she had seen.

When they arrived back at the apartment, Thane intended to give her a quick goodnight kiss and leave, but then he had to give her another longer one, then another. Finally he broke free, his whole body trembling with need. "Tru, my sweet, get in your apartment. I'll see you tomorrow for lunch. No. Make that breakfast. We'll have Greek omelets."

"Yes." In a daze Tru went in, undressed, hung up her clothes, laid out things for the next day, then went to bed, all without coming out of the aura that Thane had created. Tru accepted her fate. Thane Stoner had become her world. There never could be a more powerful love in her life.

The next morning Thane was there to pick her up and take her to breakfast, then drive her to work.

Later in the day she went directly to class. It was difficult working and going to school, but she had dropped one class that she planned to pick up in the next semester, and that had lightened her load.

She was sitting in the library taking notes with reference books strewn in front of her when she sensed someone at her side. She looked up. "Roger! What are you doing here?"

"There was no other way to speak to you. Your boyfriend is always at your apartment."

Tru stared at him as he went around the table and sat down opposite her. Had he always had that sneering smile? It appalled her to think that at that moment she couldn't see anything appealing about the man who had lived with her as her husband. "Don't throw bricks, Roger. I haven't said anything about the woman who's living with you."

His face turned an angry shade of red. He started to raise his voice, but then remembered where he was. "Don't you say anything about Heidi. She's more woman than you could ever be and as soon as the divorce is final we're getting married. And we are not living together. She has her place and I have mine."

"Goody."

"Don't get smart with me, Tru." Roger leaned across the table. "You think you've bagged a big one, don't you? But he'll never marry you. The Stoners wouldn't want a nobody like you in the family." He saw how his words had affected her, so he zeroed in for the kill. "And don't think I won't make a stink about you living with him. My lawyer says—"

"I am *not* living with him." People at nearby tables were looking their way, glowering at them. When she spoke again, her voice was low. "Stop being nasty, Roger. You're still upset because I took back the things that belonged to me. Why don't you leave? I have studying to do."

"Don't talk to me that way." This time a woman at the stacks shushed them. Roger rose to his feet, glaring around him, before looking back at Tru. "You just remember that I'll go after you and your rich sugar daddy for adultery." With that he wheeled around and strode out of the library.

"You . . . hypocrite," Tru said under her breath.

She tried to concentrate on her studies, but Roger's words kept coming back to her. He would be more than willing to drag Thane's name through the mud. Tru promised herself that she would do everything in her power to prevent that.

Thane picked her up after her last class, noting that she looked tired. "Maybe it's too much for you, coming to the university right from work."

Tru shook her head. "I get off at four and it's only a short walk to campus. It was sheer luck that allowed me to change my schedule so I only had to drop one class and can take the rest in the late afternoon and early evening. I'm through by seven forty-five."

"It's still a long day, Tru."

"So it is." She tried to smile at him.

"What's wrong? You look upset."

"Roger stopped by the library today. He wants to make sure I won't hold things up, I suppose."

"Are you keeping something from me?"

"No—what do you mean?" Tru had no intention of telling Thane what Roger had threatened to do. "Where are we eating this evening?"

"Don't think I don't know that you're trying to change the subject, lady. We'll let it rest for now, but I promise you sooner or later I'll find out what it is you're hiding from me."

"A gentleman doesn't ask a lady to reveal all her secrets," Tru said coyly, then laughed, sliding closer to Thane.

"Cute, Tru." Thane threaded his hand through hers and lifted it to his mouth, his teeth nipping at the soft skin. "You're smoking me, darling, but I'll let you get away with it this time."

"Where are we going?" Tru looked around her as they drove up a deserted canyon road.

"I have a little hideaway up here. You can study while I make dinner."

Tru looked down into the canyon from the serpentine road they were traveling into the hills. "Beautiful." When they turned into a dirt road, Tru sat up straighter, finally catching sight of a cabin sparkling like a jewel next to a mountain lake. "I've been past this area many times, but I never knew there was a lake around here."

Thane handed her her canvas carryall from the trunk and took two bags of groceries. "That's because it's a private lake."

"You own a lake." Tru grimaced at him when he laughed. A shadow of dread passed over her. Thane had so much that Roger wanted in life—recognition, money, power. She felt a fearful certainty that Roger would try to wrest something from Thane.

"Come on, daydreamer, let's go into the house. It's getting cool and damp. I'll light a fire."

Tru was delighted with the rough-hewn natural red wood interior of the spacious cabin. She looked up at the second-floor balcony.

"That's the bedroom suite up there. Since I never let anyone come here with me, I've never needed another bedroom." Thane kissed her nape before going into the kitchen and placing his groceries on the counter.

He returned to her, taking her carryall from her and leading her to the huge couch that made a semicircle in front of the fireplace. "And this is where you'll be. I'll light a fire and then get dinner started."

Thane was very businesslike as he helped her spread out her work, set a large glass of ice cold cider near her, then kissed her forehead and left her to her books.

Tru *did* get a great deal of work done, but many times she looked up to study Thane for long moments. The kitchen was open to the living room. There were no walls between them in the airy loft-like space. She smiled as she watched him whistling and cutting vegetables.

When he looked up and caught her watching him, he wiped his hand on the towel he'd tied around his waist and approached her, leaning over the back of the couch and kissing her deeply. "I'd love to keep on with this, but the cooking won't get done and neither will the studying."

After that Tru was sure she wouldn't get any in-depth work done with Thane so close. The nape of her neck prickled with awareness of him. As she sat on the couch she could hear the noises he made with the pots and pans behind her.

She picked up her notes and began to riffle through them. To her surprise she managed to make inroads on outlines for two term papers, the deadline on both of which was at the end of the week. Tru was so engrossed in what she was doing that when the hand came over her shoulder and pressed down on the paper in front of her, she jumped.

"Enough." Thane walked around to face her and closed her books. "Food's ready," he said. He bent low and pressed his mouth to hers even as he put his hands under her arms and lifted her straight up from the couch.

His strength astounded and thrilled her. It seemed very natural to place her arms around his neck and press her face to his as he carried her to the small table set in front of the bay window overlooking the lake. For a moment, after he seated her in a chair, she hung onto him. Thane was such a wonderful addition to her world, yet she knew her life was too complicated to keep him in it. She wished with all her heart that she had met him before Roger.

"Umm, nice." Thane smiled down at her, his smile fading slowly. Tru had the cloudy look in her eyes again. "Something wrong?"

"I guess I'm just hungry," she lied. How could she tell him that she had already begun to grieve for the time when they would have to part? For how could they keep on, with Roger breathing down their necks? Part of her also wondered whether what her soon-to-be ex-husband had said was true? Could she ever truly be a part of Thane Stoner's fast-lane life? And if she gave herself to him—the self she'd reclaimed after the divorce—would he subsume her? He was nothing if not an incredibly forceful man.

Suddenly there were just too many "ifs." Suddenly something told her that she and Thane could never be together, and that knowledge hurt.

Thane nodded, not believing her, wariness filling him as he ladled out the chili.

Tru waited for him to pour the wine and take the chair adjacent to hers before she picked up her spoon and sampled the chili. She blinked, then groped for her water glass. "Hot," she gasped.

Thane grinned. "Not so. That's *mild* Texas chili, ma'am. Here is the thing that will heat it up for you." He proferred a small pitcher of brownish liquid. "Throw some of this on the ground in Texas, and you'll get an oil gusher."

"You're not Texan. How would you know?" She laughed, shaking her head at the hot sauce.

"One of my frat brothers at the university was from Dallas. He taught me how to make this."

"Sue him for wrongful death," Tru wheezed as she continued to spoon the chili into her mouth.

"I knew you'd like it." Thane leaned over and kissed her cheek.

"I'll never be cold again, that's for sure." Tru grinned at him. He threw back his head and laughed.

They did the dishes together, their bodies bumping gently.

Afterwards they sat on the couch and watched the fire, sipping coffee and brandy. Thane kneaded her neck gently with his fingers. Then he removed the coffee cup from her hand and placed it beside his brandy snifter on the table. Tru faced him as though it were the most natural thing in the world. "I know what's coming and I should stop it."

"Are you going to?" Thane cupped her face in his hands, his mouth feathering kisses over the soft skin.

"No. I want this."

"So do I, Tru. I've wanted this since the moment I saw you staring at Ellen's front door, torn between joining the party and going home."

"If you'd been even a minute later we might not have met. I was about to leave."

"Wrong, my love," Thane told her, his strong arms lifting her across his lap. "I told you that we were destined to meet. No earthquake, hurricane, or act of God could have changed that."

"Powerful stuff," Tru crooned, her head lolling on her neck. Thane caressed her throat, face, and shoulders with his fevered mouth, firing her deepest emotions.

"Very." Thane uttered a curse that sounded more like a prayer as his body responded to her with speed and sensual hardening of muscle and sinew.

His fingers pressed and tested the bones of her shoulder and neck, loving the fragile strength of her frame, his hand sliding to her breast and cupping it. "You're in charge, darling." He struggled to keep his voice even, the blood thundering in his ears. "We stop if you want to, but I hope you don't." His tongue teased the corner of her mouth, then speared gently between her lips, making her moan. He pulled back at once. "Darling?"

"Thane." Tru took one of his hands and guided it back to her breast.

Thane felt his body bloom with wanting, needing, but even more, a desire to give all of himself. At the same time he knew he was receiving a priceless gift: Tru.

Their mouths and bodies fused together. Slowly Thane began to remove her clothing, beginning with her blouse. He eased it off her shoulders, then put her on her feet so that he could slide her cotton skirt off her hips.

When she was standing in front of him in bra and panties he kept her between his knees and looked up at her. "You're too lovely for words, lady mine, but your hip bones show."

"I'll fatten up." Tru had no clear idea what they were saying to each other. She only knew that she was at once more serene and more excited than she'd ever been in her life. This kind of love was brand new, a wonder never before experienced.

"I'll take care of feeding you." He nuzzled the skin of her abdomen, his tongue touching her navel before moving upward in slow, sweet exploration, the fingers of each hand accompanying his mouth as it moved over her body. He reached behind her to unhook her bra, then cupped each breast as he ministered to her nipples with his mouth. "You aren't chilled are you, darling?"

A tousled Thane looked up at her, the sensual sleepiness in his eyes making the blood pound through her body.

Tru combed her hands through the thickness of his hair, the touch electrifying her skin. "I'm very warm."

"Good." On his knees in front of her now with his back to the couch he began to nudge the panties she wore downward with his mouth, each move a caress. "You have such lovely skin, Tru."

"Thane." She clutched his head, holding him closer to her.

She had a sensation of flying as he surged to his feet taking her with him, holding her so that her feet were off the ground but their mouths were level and touching as he strode across the room and up the stairs to the loft and the king-sized bed awaiting them.

Thane placed her face down on the bed and finished removing the lace-edged panties, placing soft kisses along her spine, nipping gently at her buttocks, his hands feathering over her in questing gentleness.

Tru was excited, the fine hairs on her body quivering to sensuous alertness. Never had she experienced such ballooning joy. Her hands curled into the sheet under her as wave after wave of feeling assaulted her.

Tru wiggled around so that she was on her back. She needed to hold him to give to him.

"What's wrong, darling? Did I make you uncomfortable?"

"No. I wanted to look at you." She let her hands slide over him, and as she touched his arousal, her fingers clenched and unclenched caressingly.

"God. I see what you mean." Thane closed his eyes, letting her become the aggressor, delighting in the new sensations she was engendering, feeling enervated and almighty at once under her touch. "Did you invent lovemaking, lady?"

"Maybe." She laughed out loud with the sheer joy of loving him, holding him, wanting him.

"Tru."

"Thane."

They couldn't touch each other enough. Fevered hands and mouths were everywhere, creating a hot cyclone of feeling that lifted them upward.

"Ah," Thane groaned hoarsely.

"More." Passion quivered through Tru as she felt her being splice to his.

"No more." Thane's every pore shook with the need of her. "I can't hold back, darling."

His face slid down her body so that he could enter her with the most intimate of caresses. When she cried out, he stared up at her passion-glazed expression and knew with the unerring savvy of the true lover that no one had ever made her feel like this. Happier than he'd ever been, to see that he could give her a unique pleasure, he said, "No woman has ever thrilled me as you have, angel. I want to keep you with me always." The words calmed their emotional hurricane, and Thane welcomed it because he wanted their first time to be perfect for her, sweet and slow, caring and loving.

Suddenly, though, Roger's face took shape before Tru's eyes. Struggling to bury the image, she clung to Thane. "Don't talk about always or forever," she cried.

"Tru! Don't! You're thinking of him now. I can feel it. I am not Roger Hubbard."

"You're nothing like him, Thane."

"Then don't compare what we have to what you had with him."

"I don't. Not really." Tru didn't feel she could explain her fear that Roger would do something to spoil what she and Thane had—not here, not now. It would mean putting a stop to their lovemaking, and at this moment she felt she'd rather die than do that. She freed herself from him and lifted herself up on one elbow so that she could look into his eyes. "You're staring at me."

"You have the most wonderful body. I knew that even when you were dressed, but now . . ." Thane shook his head, his fingers touching her before he looked back at her. "But that isn't what you wanted to say to me. Is it?"

"No. I wanted to tell you that I could never compare you to Roger. It would be impossible. Since you came into my life, I've rarely thought of him. It was as though you swept him from my mind. And I'm glad." Tru leaned forward so that her nipples grazed his chest. "I've felt more like a woman at your side than I *ever* did with Roger."

"Tru, you've just sent my ego through the roof. You have the power to make me or break me, lady. Remember that, will you?" He touched her tenderly, his fingers sliding over her skin.

"And you do the same to me." Tru smiled at him, hoping she was masking the hollowness of her words. Yes, everything she'd told him was true. But that hadn't been all. There were fears she couldn't voice, premonitions she couldn't share with him. "Is this just a pause or are we going to quit loving altogether?"

"Just a pause. We don't want to rush it, do we?" Thane reached for her, noting the shadow that flashed across her eyes. So much of Tru was hidden from him, and he wanted to know it all. But not now. He urged her back against the pillows again, his mouth homing in on her neck. "I intend to make love to you all night."

"No problem." Tru's husky laugh reached out to him. "I've done so much work that I can afford the time."

"Brat. And stop wriggling like that. I refuse to rush our very first time together. When we're old and bent over, I'll look at you and wink and mention

'the time at the cabin,' and you'll remember this
very clearly, thanks to me."

Tru threw her arms around his neck, hiding her
face, not wanting him to see her consternation. If
only he'd stop talking about the future and concentrate on the here and now! That's all they had. "I
thought we weren't going to talk any more."

"Oh, lady, we've only just *begun* talking—only now
we do it with our bodies."

Tru's hands dug through his hair, pulling him
close to her.

Thane's body was in chaos. He throbbed with the
need of her. She belonged to him and he'd never let
her go.

He pulled back, studying her lower body, the tri-
angle of dark blond hair. Then he pressed his face
there, adoring her, making a silent covenant to her
that he intended to voice later. His tongue touched
her again and again, this time rhythmically imitat-
ing the thrusts of his lower body. Thane blew gently,
holding her when her body bucked in response, but
not releasing her. His caresses became more insis-
tent, drawing from her the same physical commit-
ment he was making to her.

Tru had never felt so magnetized. It was as though
she had taken on part of Thane, and he part of her.
"I love you."

"Oh, darling, and how I love you."

Tru wanted to deny she'd said it when she saw
Thane's eyes glittering in triumph. It was happening too fast. Would it disappear as quickly? But
when he entered her, her mind went blank, all of
her reservations vanished, and she loved her man to
the exclusion of all else. Nothing intruded, nothing
came between them.

It seemed as if the force of their passion took

them and spilled them off the planet into a world of kaleidoscopic emotion and delight.

For long moments after, they held each other in quiet joy.

"Tru?"

"Hmm?"

"Was it wonderful for you, darling?"

"Better than wonderful."

"Are you happy?"

"There is no way to describe it, Thane. I never dreamed two people could create such marvels."

"Neither did I."

"I can think of a hundred things to say, but they all seem like clichés."

Thane shook his head and gathered her close to him. "Rest."

Tru nodded and closed her eyes.

In the night, Thane woke her and they made love again. This time, it was somehow both a new yet familiar joy.

"This will never change in our life, love, not when we're ninety."

Tru held him when he slept, those words running round and round in her head. Who would be the lucky woman still holding this man when he was ninety? A tear slid down her cheek.

Four

Three weeks after their tryst at Thane's place in the mountains Tru felt caught in a web of her own making. Every day she resolved to tell Thane that she had to end their affair, that they were going too fast, that she needed to back off a bit until her divorce came through many months hence. But each night when she saw him, her good intentions went out the window and the intensity of their feelings for one another burgeoned until there was no room left for caution.

"I won't be able to see you until late tomorrow, love," Thane told her one night as he was leaving her, regret filling him as it always did at their parting. He wanted to be with her all the time, wake up with her in the morning, listen to music with her, go to the ball game with her. Leaving her bothered him more than he'd thought anything could. "I've called a staff meeting for tomorrow, and if this one is like the others, it will go on well past the dinner hour." Thane ran his hand through the thickness of her hair, loving the silkiness of it. "I love your hair, darling. I look forward to the time when I'll have it wrapped around my neck every night . . . when we're living together."

"Thane," Tru sobbed, laying her cheek against his chest, her arms around him.

"I'm not going to be patient much longer, my love. I hate anything that comes between us . . . damn this meeting!"

"I understand about your work. A man's work has to come first."

"It used to. Now you do."

A wrenching sadness tore through Tru at the thought that she wouldn't be seeing him for dinner the following evening. "You don't have to come after the meeting. You'll probably want to go home and go to bed," she told him bravely.

"Stupid lady. I'll be here.'" He kissed her nose and left.

She was so tempted to call him back and beg him to stay the night that she closed and locked her door quickly and pressed herself against it. They'd been scrupulous about separating every night, though after making love, it wasn't easy. Still, Tru had insisted and Thane had honored her wish, assuming she was concerned about jeopardizing her position in the divorce.

The next day her job seemed interminable, her classes incomprehensible. The simplest task jangled her nerves. More than once Tru had to ask someone to repeat what he'd said. Everything seemed impossible—all because she wouldn't be seeing Thane for lunch or dinner.

That evening she felt weary to the bone when she returned to her apartment. But she was greeted by something that made her spirits rise, a letter from Maggie telling her that she'd had amniocentesis and now knew that her baby was a girl. Tru laughed and cried at the same time, promising herself that she would write Maggie first thing tomorrow. She made a quick omelet and decided to grab a nap so she would be rested when, and if, Thane came by.

She had finished her small meal, cleaned up and was just getting out of the shower, cocooned in a terry cloth bath sheet, when the door bell rang. "Thane!" He was early. Without thinking, she rushed to the door and flung it open, the welcoming smile dying on her face. "Roger! What do you want?"

"How charming, Tru." Roger pushed past her into the room, looking around him. "It's small." There was satisfaction in his voice.

"And it's mine. So leave."

"Not before I get a few things said." Roger went over to the couch and sat down, stretching his legs out in front of him, then staring up at her. "You look very fetching in your towel. Perhaps you'd like to play house for an hour or two."

Tru stalked to the kitchen, took the rolling pin out of the drawer and went back to him. "How would you like your skull bashed in? You disgust me and you don't have any right to be here. So unless you want me to have the superintendent throw you out, you'd better state your business and then leave."

Roger's face turned a mottled red, his mouth thinning. "You've gotten tough, haven't you?"

"I had to or I wouldn't have survived your steamrolling and shabby treatment. Cheating and lying upset my system." She brandished the rolling pin when he started to rise. "Say what you've come to say and get out of here."

"All right, but I'm glad I won't be married to you much longer."

"You couldn't be happier about that than I am. Talk fast."

"You won't be getting a penny out of me." Roger's voice was vitriolic.

"Oh? My lawyer seems to think that you owe me something for the education that you received while I paid the bills. The fact that you didn't have the decency to take a part-time job when you were in school doesn't say much for you either, David says."

Roger inhaled an angry breath and jumped to his feet. "And my lawyer says that since you have been consorting in such an unseemly way with another man while still married to me, we can prove that you were unfaithful to me. And since you're more than likely to be supported by him after we break up, the judge will probably find in my favor."

"What? How can you say such a thing? *You* were the one who was unfaithful to *me* with that woman you're living with now."

"You don't know what you're talking about."

"Shut up, Roger, you make me ill."

His face darkened. "I have pictures of him coming out of here at all hours of the night and I know you spent a weekend with him out of town. You don't have any pictures of me with Heidi."

"You creep. You . . . scum." Tru shook the rolling pin at him when he faced her triumphantly.

"Just remember that you can talk all you want about my lady friend and me, but you don't have any proof to back it up." Roger patted his breast pocket. "I do. You know, I don't think your rich boyfriend will like seeing his name plastered all over the tabloids. He's a pretty well-known person from a prestigious family. They might get a little uptight about the adverse publicity. His career might suffer, and I hear he's got political ambitions—"

"You worm," Tru shouted. She could feel the blood draining from her face as she pictured the situation that Roger was spelling out for her. She couldn't let that happen. She loved Thane.

Roger rose. "So you tell that lawyer of yours that

you don't need anything, *if* you want to protect your fancy boyfriend."

Tru stared at him blindly, the rolling pin slipping from her grasp and dropping with a thud to the floor.

Roger stared back, a hard smile on his face, before he took two quick steps to her, lifted his hand and struck her across the face. "And don't you ever threaten me again."

Tru's head snapped back as she spun and fell against the couch, her hand flying to her stinging cheek.

Roger strode to the door, flinging it open, then slamming it behind him.

Tru sat there staring at the wall.

As she put a hand up to the painful throbbing in her face, she started to shiver. Dazedly, she realized that she was still wrapped in the damp towel. She had to dress, but it was an effort even to move.

Roger would do what he promised, she knew. He was a man who always remembered a slight and he'd clearly felt slighted when he learned of her relationship with Thane, even though *he'd* abandoned her. But somehow, Tru realized, in his warped mind Roger still thought of her as his property. He'd always been extremely possessive. Somehow it all made a contorted kind of sense.

She shuddered as she dressed in her bedroom and thought about what he'd said. Then she went to the bathroom to put a cold compress on her cheek. Later, when she removed the compress, she noted that her skin was red and puffy with the beginnings of a bruise. So she applied a heavy coating of makeup to mask it.

For the first time that day she hoped that Thane wouldn't visit her.

Tru spent long hours with her textbooks studying

and making notes, but when she found herself reading the same sentence over and over again, she put her things away. Her face was throbbing like a toothache.

Smothering a yawn with her hand she stared at her watch in amazement. Eleven o'clock! Surely, Thane wouldn't be coming tonight. Torn between sadness and relief, she readied herself for sleep. When the doorbell rang just as she was about to get into bed, she was stunned. Hustling to the front door she paused in front of the door. "Who is it?"

"Tru, darling. It's Thane. Open up."

She slipped the bolts and turned the key. As soon as the door was open a crack, Thane reached for her. Holding her, he leaned back against the door shutting it with his shoulder. "I missed you." He kissed her, rubbing his mouth against hers before delving deeply with his tongue. One of his hands clasped her waist, the other feathered over her breasts, caressing and pressing gently, up to her neck and ears, before cupping her chin. His mouth didn't lift from hers until his questing fingers touched something that set off an alarm in him. "What's this? Did you fall? Why is your face swollen?" He could feel the smile freeze on his face when her eyes slid away from his. "Tru! What is it?"

Thane scooped her up into his arms and carried her into the living room, setting her down at the end of the couch and switching on the lamp nearest her. "Let me look at that." With a tender but firm touch he turned her face to the light. "Dear Lord. What happened? Tell me."

"No," Tru whispered.

"Dammit, Tru, tell me." He sat down next to her and lifted her onto his lap. "I have to know. Did you fall?"

"No." Thoughts skidded around her brain like marbles across a polished wood floor; she searched among them for something to tell him.

Thane felt as if he weren't getting enough oxygen even though his heart was pounding fiercely. "Did someone strike you?" The hoarse intensity of his voice brought her frightened gaze to him. "Who?"

"No."

"Tell me."

"He wouldn't have done it if I hadn't threatened him. . . ." Tru rushed her words, her hands clutching his shirt front, her eyes pleading with him.

"Who hit you?"

"Roger, but he was angry because—"

Thane surged to his feet, still holding her close to his chest, his body shaking. He had never felt such fury. It closed his throat, made it impossible for him to breathe.

"Thane?"

He stormed into her bedroom and placed her on the bed. "He struck you! Damn his soul to hell!"

"No, no, Thane, please, it's not important. Don't be angry. It doesn't even hurt that much."

"Damn him." Thane touched her face. "I want this examined by a doctor."

"Don't be silly. The mark will be gone in a couple of days."

"No, it won't. He socked you." His fingers feathered over her cheek. "This was no open-handed slap. He should never have touched you, let alone done this." He ground his teeth together. "I'll have his hide!"

"No, you must promise me that you won't do anything. You must stay away from Roger. Swear you will." She panicked and clutched at him desperately. "Let it go, Thane. It isn't important." Tru's hands fluttered over him, anguish swelling in her voice.

"Don't you worry about a thing." Thane kissed the palm of her hand, hiding his face there for a moment. He would take care of Hubbard and the man would rue the day he ever struck Tru. But Thane had no intention of upsetting her about it.

He looked up at her and smiled lazily. "Now, my darling, I'm putting you to bed, then I'm joining you. I think you've had enough excitement for one evening. You could have nightmares from this, and if you do I'll be there."

"Thane, you can't stay," she told him faintly, wanting him to remain with her, but fearing Roger, remembering his vicious threats.

"No arguing. It won't do you any good." Thane placed her under the covers. "Scoot over. You don't get the middle of the bed tonight." Thane smiled down at her.

"I think sleeping in the center is the only way possible in this bed. Every night I slide into the middle anyway because the mattress sags."

"Sounds wonderful." He grinned at her, noting that some of the strain had left her face when she smiled back at him. His eyes touched the swollen side of her face and he swallowed a curse. His insides were still boiling but he made every effort to hide it from her.

Tru stared up at him as he undressed, feeling no discomfort. Rather she was eager to look at the man she loved. She longed to gaze at his body, to feel him next to her, and though a voice inside warned her to be careful, she had to ignore it.

"Why, darling, you embarrass me."

She laughed up at him as he stood before her, naked. "You're not at all embarrassed."

"No, I'm not. I'm delighted that you're looking at me because I sure as hell want the same privilege." He slipped into bed beside her and cuddled her close to him, his own hand easing the nightgown from her. "You don't mind, do you?"

Tru shook her head, reeling with the wonder of lying beside him.

When she was as naked as he, Thane studied her, his hand trembling as he touched her. "You're so beautiful, Tru."

"And you are too."

He laughed and hugged her to him. "You're a darling." Thane reached up and turned off the light over the bed. "You're safe now, sweetheart. Incidentally, I like this bed."

"It's too short for you."

Thane shifted her so that her head was on his shoulder. "Sleep now, love."

Stunned, Tru tried to see his features in the darkened room. "Aren't you going to make love to me?"

"I thought you might prefer to rest."

"Maybe it's not wise for us to sleep together because of the divorce." Tru still couldn't bring herself to tell Thane what Roger had said and how he'd frightened her. "But as long as we're here, together, I would like to make love with you."

"God, I want that too, lamb." Thane began kissing her, his mouth frantic on her body.

"Thane, I want you so much."

"And I love you and want you with me always."

She felt engulfed by joy, but the sharp knowledge of the futility of their relationship cut through her like a knife. What they both wanted—to be together—simply could not be.

That night Tru's caresses had a frenzy to them. Thane sensed her urgency and wanted to question her, but the words died at his lips under her sensuous onslaught.

Love coursed through them. There was no higher plane than the one they ascended to, entwined in each other's arms. They lay as though under an avalanche of feeling, buried in the wanting and the need.

"Never did I know that life held such wonder." Tru breathed as she felt him part her legs again and slide between them. "I do love you."

When Thane opened his eyes the next morning, he blinked once, then realized where he was; the warm weight pressed against his side had the power to excite him again, even though they'd made love three times in the night. He eased himself around so that he could see her better, studying the delicate bone structure of her face and her pearly skin.

Her lips, parted softly in sleep, looked kissable and inviting and he didn't resist. When she moaned and slanted her mouth across his, his heart kicked out of rhythm. He let his hand rub slowly over her satiny form. "Tru? Open your eyes. I want to look into them when I say this."

"Sleepy." Her mouth curved in a grin even as her lids lifted. "Say what? Hello."

"Hello, darling. Will you marry me?"

Tru's eyes widened as she stared up at him. "I'm not divorced."

Thane saw the panic in her eyes. Never had he imagined that when he finally asked the woman of his choice this question, her face would look like this. "You don't have to act as though I asked you to walk the plank." His mouth nuzzled her neck. "Just say yes."

Tru clutched him, hiding her face on his shoulder. "Thane, we can't think of marriage yet. Give me time."

"Dammit, Tru, you told me you loved me and you know how I feel about you."

She stroked his cheek, trying to mask the turmoil that was churning inside her. "I know. But could you give me a little time?"

Without answering he moved to the edge of the bed, bringing her with him. "You get the bathroom first. I'll make the bed."

Tru tried to smile at him as she got up, but then saw the thrust of his jaw, the smoldering hurt in his eyes.

Thane smacked the pillows and yanked at the sheets, ignoring Tru when she glided to the bathroom.

By the time Thane showered he felt more in control, vowing to himself that he would break down whatever barriers Tru had erected between them. Dammit, she loved him! She'd told him so a hundred times.

Tru breathed a sigh of relief when she felt his arms slide around her waist as she was cooking eggs. She turned with the spatula still in her hand and lifted her mouth to his. "Thane. I *do* love you."

"I love you, too, pretty lady." Nothing was going to separate them! He would see to that. None of her maneuvering to keep them apart until the divorce was final would make a particle of difference.

They fed each other toast and bits of scrambled egg and because they lingered, Tru was almost late for work.

"You don't care because you can't be fired," she told Thane later, pushing away from him as they sat in his car in front of her building.

"If they fire you, I'll hire you as my personal assistant." He kissed her neck, making soft animal sounds against her skin. "I don't know why I didn't do that in the first place."

"And I suppose you'd be doing this all day? Your business would go down the drain. Will you let me go?"

"Of course we'd be doing this all day. I'd have to have *some* privileges." He frowned at her. "I don't want to let you go."

"Thane," Tru wailed.

"All right. I'll pick you up after your class and we'll get something to eat."

Tru was about to tell him that class had been canceled and that she would be getting out early, but she thought better of it.

All day long she laid plans about how she was going to handle the dilemma Roger presented to her. She went through one scenario after another, but only one solution surfaced. She would have to leave California . . . leave Thane. She would get out of Los Angeles area at least until after her divorce was final. That was the only way to put a stop to Roger's threats to Thane's good name. Then . . . after the divorce she could return.

She decided to go home and call Maggie and see what the job market was like in New York. She was sure she could get back to the campus before Thane arrived to get her. Thane! Thane! The thought of leaving him weighed heavy on her soul. It seemed such an effort to pick up the phone and punch in her friends number.

"It's just that I feel I should get away," she told Maggie. "Roger is causing trouble. He doesn't want to give me any money and he could get nasty. I don't want that, I just want to be free of him."

"Ellen says that you've been seeing Thane Stoner."

"I've been seeing him."

"That's pretty cryptic, old friend." Maggie chuckled. "You may not want to tell me about it, Tru, but I'll get it out of you when you come here."

Tru smiled to herself, feeling warmed and comforted. She and Maggie had always had a very special relationship, even closer than the one she had with Ellen. "If the job market is good I'll come there. Do you know of any openings?"

"I certainly do," Maggie answered gleefully. "I started

an answering service in my home and, believe it or not, it's been growing by leaps and bounds. I thought it would be a good way to help out financially without leaving the house after the baby is born. Now I'm beginning to think I took on too much. It would be wonderful if you could come here and we could be partners. Then I could shift some of the load to you."

"You're not just making up something to help me?"

"Honest Injun, I need you, friend."

Tru felt teary as she listened to Maggie. "It would be an answer to all my troubles."

"For me too, Tru. I've missed you and Ellen so much."

"And we've missed you." Tru laughed with her friend, wiping a tear from her cheek.

"Oh Tru, you'll love it in our new place. We inherited a brownstone from one of Ted's aunts and there's plenty of room for you here. You can have your own suite, and we'll see each other every day."

"Maggie." Emotion closed Tru's throat for a moment.

"Are you crying? Don't you dare. You'll get me started and I cry buckets at the drop of a hat since I became pregnant. Now stop it. Everything will be fine. You'll see."

"I know." Tru's heart plummeted as she pictured herself three thousand miles from Thane.

"Are you going to tell Ellen where you'll be? And don't try to pretend you're not running away from something bigger than Roger, because you are. I know you too well."

"Smarty. I am, but I don't think I can talk about it yet." Tru swallowed painfully. "I'll . . . I'll tell Ellen and my lawyer that I'm coming to you, but no one else."

After she hung up, Tru felt as if the die had been cast. There was no going back. If she was to protect Thane from Roger, she had to disappear so that her former husband couldn't smear Thane's good name with his nasty allegations.

After rinsing her face with cold water and redoing her makeup, she left the apartment and returned to the campus.

That night she didn't even suggest that Thane leave, and their lovemaking was fiercer than ever before.

"I love you," Thane crooned to her over and over again. "Would you like to go to San Francisco with me next Wednesday? I'll be driving back on Thursday. We could sightsee and have dinner. It would be good for you to get away, Tru."

"I have a midterm then, Thane. I can't miss it," she told him truthfully. She didn't tell him that she was already planning to leave while he was out of town. Instead she clung to him. "When I'm near you, I'm happy."

"Darling!" Thane soothed her. "We'll go to San Francisco someday soon and stay longer. I want to take you everywhere . . . all over the world."

"Yes."

The next few days Tru spent every free moment with Thane, while trying to keep a wary eye out for Roger. She had no intention of taking the chance of him striking at her again. The strain of knowing she was leaving Thane and worry about Roger's next move began to tell on her. The slightest thing startled her.

Thane noticed her growing edginess, putting it down to the strain of the divorce, her fear of Roger. And every time Thane mentioned it, he ground his teeth in outrage.

That week Thane decided to do something about

Roger. He remembered where Tru had said he worked, and it pleased him to no end that the owner of the firm had been a classmate of his. Thane went directly to the president's office when he arrived at the company.

"Thanks, Jim. I only want to speak to the creep for a minute."

"I don't like the look in your eye, so I hope you won't mind if I'm not around when you find Hubbard." Jim Feldman grimaced at his fraternity brother. "And please believe I'll bill you for any damage."

"No problem," Thane told him grimly.

When he entered the large office with about twenty desks, he had to ask where Hubbard was. Thane approached the desk that had been pointed out to him. "Hubbard? Roger Hubbard?"

"Yes." Roger looked up, a smile drying on his face.

"That's right. You know who I am, don't you?" Thane reached down and gripped his shirt front, pulling him out of his chair and smacking him across the jaw.

Roger fell back into his chair again, his hand coming up to massage his face. "I could have you arrested."

"Feel free. But let me tell you something. If you ever go near Tru again I'll come back and beat the hell out of you." Thane looked down at him, ignoring the gasps from workers around him. "Remember what I said." He strolled up the aisle of desks, barely aware of the people who scurried out of his way.

Five

Tru spent the next week taking care of personal business for the move to New York.

"David, it won't be a problem, will it?"

David Wilson studied the strained face of his client. "No, but I can tell you right now that my life will be in danger from Thane Stoner. I've known him since our summer camp days and he's tough. He'll put the pressure on to find you."

"But you won't tell him?"

"Lawyer-client confidentiality. Don't worry, Tru, things will work out, even though I don't think you need to go to New York. I think we can fight Hubbard on this."

"But in the meantime Thane's name will be dragged through the mud."

"You don't know Thane if you think that would bother him. Of course, he might break Hubbard's head, but he wouldn't be upset about the publicity, and you shouldn't be either."

Tru shook her head. "I'm leaving. I can't let it come to that."

David shrugged and shook his head. "Have it your way, Tru."

On the day that Thane was to drive to San Francisco, Tru almost couldn't keep herself from collapsing into his arms, telling him everything and begging him to take her with him.

They laughed together and talked all through breakfast, washing up the few dishes and kissing each other constantly.

"You have classes today. Right?"

"Some," Tru dissembled. She had already talked to her professors about leaving and made sure that her credits could be transferred to a university in New York.

They kissed good-bye in the apartment because even though Tru didn't tell Thane, she was worried that Roger might be outside photographing if they kissed on the street. Her skin crawled at the idea.

"I'll come right here tomorrow night, darling." Thane gave her a lingering kiss. It flashed through his mind that there was more sadness at their parting in her eyes. "Are you all right, Tru?"

"Oh yes. I just hate good-byes."

"So do I, now."

After he left, she packed like an automaton, arranging with Ellen to have some of her things stored. She wore a hat and dark glasses to the airport, dressing in nondescript clothes and buying a ticket for herself under an assumed name. She wanted to make it difficult if not impossible, to be found.

The plane was crowded but Tru scarcely noticed. She stared out the window blindly for the entire trip, refusing all food and drink.

When they arrived in Chicago, she went to the ladies' room and changed clothes, twisting her hair into a bun.

She left the terminal she was in and went to another in the huge complex of O'Hare Airport. There she bought a ticket on another airline for the flight to New York.

When the plane left the ground it carried a Mary G. Wayland on board, the dry-eyed woman staring out the window into the thick clouds.

Tru had left him! No note, no phone call, no explanation. She'd just cleaned out her apartment and vanished. No one at the university or the Pillor Building knew where she was.

When Thane went to the Sandilins, he could tell right away that Ellen knew where Tru had gone.

"No way can I tell you, Thane. I gave Tru my word. I won't break it, not even for you."

Thane swallowed, hating the pitying looks he was getting from the family that had been so aware of his good fortune in the past. "Forget it," he said, and left in a rush, his tires squealing as he tore down the drive onto the main road.

The next day Thane sent for the private investigator he'd employed more than once before—the last time being when Roger had taken Tru's things. He gave him as much information as he had and a picture of her that had been taken at Maggie's wedding. "I'll try to find her," Billy began, then studied the bleak face that Thane turned to him. "I'll get back to you as soon as I can."

Billy called three weeks later. "I think I've found her in New York. She's living in a brownstone with three other people." Billy paused and Thane could hear him rustling papers. "An older woman who probably owns the house and another young woman and a guy about the same age. Do you want me to check them out?"

"Never mind that. I'm flying to New York. Thanks, Billy."

"That's what you pay me for, Mr. Stoner."

It was late the same day when Thane checked into the Pierre in New York. He decided to eat and then hit the sack, so that he'd be ready to see her first thing the next morning.

Visions of Tru—laughing, crying, lost in cloudy thoughts, shaking her fist at him in mock anger— danced in his dreams. He woke the next morning at seven, feeling as though he hadn't slept at all.

After a quick breakfast in the coffee shop downstairs, he found his rented car and followed the directions that Billy had given him to the brownstone in Greenwich Village. It was shortly after eight-thirty when he parked the car across the street from the door with number 87 above it.

Just about nine the door opened and a tall, laughing man came out and turned at the top step.

Thane straightened when he saw Tru standing beside the man, smiling.

When the man leaned down and kissed her, she put her arms around his neck and hugged him back.

Thane's world exploded. He was so angry that if he had faced Tru in that moment, he might have killed her. Instead, he spun the car around and drove back to the hotel to sit in his room and stare at the wall.

He stayed like that for two hours. When he finally returned to the world of the living, he dialed the number Billy had given him. A woman's voice with a heavy Spanish accent answered.

"No, señor, there is no Mrs. Hubbard here, only Mrs. Mason. Would you like to speak to her? Mr. Mason will be home later."

Thane replaced the receiver. That was as far as he

wanted to probe into Tru Hubbard's life—or was it Tru Mason now?

He flew back to California that afternoon. From the Los Angeles terminal he called the model he'd been dating before he'd met Tru. He made a date with her for that evening.

Tru was content in New York. Her time was filled with Maggie and Maggie's answering service, which ate up most of their daylight hours. She and Maggie made a point of taking a long walk at the noon hour, then eating a light lunch. Tru's life was beginning to take on a whole new set of patterns, most of them exceedingly pleasant.

Of course, the nights were interminable at first, but after a few weeks the pain and tension began to ease. In a few months' time she was actually able to converse and laugh with people in a natural way, and found herself getting as much as five or six hours of sleep a night.

Tru began to experience a feeling of renewed self-confidence, largely due to the fact that she was able to go as long as three hours at a time without thinking of Thane. Even planning for the future seemed possible now.

Maggie and Tom had been wonderful from the first day when they'd met her at the airport, embraced her and welcomed her like a prodigal daughter. Their friendship became the foundation upon which she set about rebuilding her life, gathering strength each day.

Right after her arrival from California she had begun learning the answering service business.

"I never thought it would mushroom like this, Tru. I don't think Tom guessed it would either."

"Oh, I don't know about that, Maggie. He's awfully proud of you."

Maggie smiled and nodded. "I think it was his confidence in me that gave me the courage to begin." Maggie pulled a paper toward her and pointed to the list of names. "We don't deal with all-night companies or doctors or anything like that. Most of our customers are small businesses with personnel who are on the road selling the product, so they need someone to monitor the phone calls and messages. It's beneficial to us to know something about the companies we deal with. That way we can answer whatever questions are put to us." Maggie paused and gazed at her friend warmly. "It's going to be great having you with me."

"For me too."

Maggie looked back at the paper in her hand. "We are cheaper to maintain for these small outfits than hiring full-time help, and they don't need to pay us benefits."

One morning several weeks later as they were breakfasting with Tom, Maggie told Tru, "I can't believe how fast you've picked everything up!"

"Work her to death, love, the way you do me on the weekends." Tom had kissed his wife good-bye, effectively sealing her sputtering protests.

Then Tom kissed Tru on the top of the head and whispered, "I'm glad you're here. She has missed her mousketeers."

"That's musketeers, Tom, and you know it." Tru had grinned. She couldn't help but admire the strength and good humor of Tom and Maggie's marriage. They were perfect for each other.

As the days passed Tru felt more comfortable with the business and was able to take more and more of the burden of it from Maggie's shoulders so that the mother-to-be had time to rest.

The weeks flew by like the wind, it seemed to Tru. Each morning she'd breakfast in her suite of rooms on the third floor, which included a kitchenette and sitting room, and then go down when she judged that Tom had left for work. Tru felt that the couple needed some private time, and she had insisted on eating the morning meal in her own rooms after the first day, despite Maggie's protests.

"Tom thinks you're avoiding him when you don't join us for breakfast." Maggie frowned at her friend as they went into the large workroom at the back of the brownstone that had once been servant's quarters before Tom and Maggie had begun renovations.

"Fiddlesticks, Maggie. He sees me enough," Tru said before playing back the messages collected from calls that had come in before they started work.

"I guess he's still a little worried about you. . . . I guess because I told him about Thane. . . ."

"Maggie!" Tru said. But she wasn't really upset that her friend had let Tom know the bare facts about the ill-fated relationship. In a way it made things easier for her, as long as she didn't have to do the explaining.

"Anyway," Maggie continued, "you know Tom—he's kind of taken the matter into his own hands." She paused before hurrying on. "He's invited a friend from the law firm over for dinner tonight, a bachelor friend."

Tru groaned inwardly but forced herself to be grateful about Tom's well-intentioned matchmaking. That night she struggled very hard to be relaxed, but every time she looked at Len Doran, Thane's rugged face appeared in place of the regular features of the other man.

Twice more Tom brought someone home, and each time the evening was pleasant. But always Thane Stoner was a silent member of the gathering, intruding and taking the place of the guest in Tru's mind. No matter how often she told herself to put that part of her life behind her until the divorce was final, memories of Thane returned.

Time passed and the threesome was happy. Maggie grew, the other two watching over her lovingly.

"Now that I'm in my eighth month I feel like an elephant," Maggie told Tom and Tru one summer evening after dinner. Maggie rolled her eyes at her friend as Tru pushed her down into her chair when she tried to clear the table. Tru paused with her shoulder propped against the swinging door between the kitchen and dining room, balancing plates and cups and saucers, and shook her head. "More like a hippo. What do you think, Tom?"

Tom studied his wife, chin in hand. "More like a rhino.

"You two are awful," Maggie wailed.

Four days past what the doctor said was Maggie's probable due date, Tru rushed her friend to the hospital in a taxi cab after calling Tom and Doctor Winstead to meet them there.

With a minimum of fuss, Margaret Ellen Mason came into the world, delighting her mother, father, and godmother-to-be.

Maggie and the baby came home two days later, along with a nurse whom they'd engaged to help care for little Margaret. But since Tru was so eager to do what was needed, she took over for the nurse after the first week.

The whole situation was ideal. Maggie and Tru would bring the portable crib into the office, and while the baby slept, they worked. Tru insisted that Maggie do very little at first and use the foldaway bed Tom had put in the office whenever she got tired out.

"And don't try to push it, Maggie. You can oversee the business from the bed."

"I don't need to supervise you. You know more than I do!"

"So lie down and close your eyes."

Soon it was September, and the leaves were just beginning to turn, the days growing shorter and the nights chillier. But the large brownstone with the brick sidewalk in front was cozy and warm.

"Mel is beautiful," Tom announced one evening when he was lying on the living room floor with the baby on his chest.

"Why do you have to shorten her name?" Maggie asked him. "Now I'm starting to call her that."

"Good. Margaret Ellen is too long a name for such a tiny lady. And one Maggie is enough for any house."

"Mel it is." Tru laughed at Maggie when she grimaced.

"Godmothers are supposed to side with the mothers."

Tru set her coffee cup on the table in front of the couch and looked at her two friends. It was good to be with them. "I agree with Tom." She got down on her knees and cooed in the baby's laughing face. "My godchild is beautiful."

"You say that because she has the same coloring as you and Tom."

"Of course," Tru giggled with Maggie.

Tom sat up with the baby, cradling her in his arm. "Tru," he said, suddenly all seriousness. "I asked Maggie if she would go to a convention with me in Bermuda. It's only three days. She thinks we'd be imposing to ask you to care for Mel."

Tru glared at her friend. "Don't be foolish. I'd love to. She's on a bottle, so that's no problem. I've cared for her right by your side, step by step, ever since you brought her home. So would you please go. I'll have Mrs. Diaz to rely on if things get hairy, which I don't foresee." Tru just knew that with the help of the cleaning woman who came every morning everything would be fine. "So what's the problem?"

"You're a darling." Maggie's eyes filled with tears.

Tom rose to his feet. "I'm going to put Mel to bed, but I'll be right back. Maggie and I want to discuss something with you, Tru."

Tru looked at her friend inquiringly, but Maggie shook her head. "Let's wait until Tom gets back. He's the lawyer in the family."

When Tom came back, he sat down next to his wife, then looked across at Tru. "I've had papers drawn up making you Mel's legal guardian in case anything happens to us. They also appoint you trustee of whatever we leave her. Is that okay with you, Tru?"

"Yes, but I wish you wouldn't talk that way," she said, shuddering. "It gives me the creeps."

"It's a formality, Tru. But it would make us feel better when we go away." Maggie kissed her husband's cheek. "Neither of us has any family, Tru. We discussed this even before you came to New York."

Tom nodded, smiling at Tru. "You can close your mouth now. Wouldn't want a bug to fly in." He opened a briefcase he's set on the table in front of him when he'd come back from putting the baby to bed. "I have papers here that give you full rights as her guardian. These even pave the way for you to adopt her as your own and give her your name. We want Mel to be well protected."

"Sounds as though you've thought of everything. Tom, you're so damned practical." Tru grimaced at the briefcase. "Now put that away and let's listen to some music."

"Here. I want you to keep a copy of this document. The other will be filed with the firm."

"All right. Now can we drop this?" Tru begged.

Three weeks later Tru said good-bye to them in the foyer of the brownstone because she was holding the baby and didn't want Mel to get a blast of chill October air.

Tru was tired that night. And Mel, sensing that something was different, was more fractious than usual. At bedtime Tru had to fuss with her, change her again, sit in the antique rocker in the living room, and read her nursery rhymes while Mel lay there blinking up at her yawning godmother.

Once Mel was asleep Tru didn't wait up to watch the eleven o'clock news, but went right to bed herself. She was asleep shortly after her head touched the pillow.

The next morning, the baby woke at six o'clock feeding. Tru decided to give her her bottle on the couch in her small sitting room and watch the morning news on television at the same time.

At first, the commentator's words didn't register. Tru saw pictures on the screen of an airplane crash in which thirty-nine people had died. Fifty-eight had apparently survived the crash at the Bermuda airport.

Bermuda! Her agitation must have communicated itself to the baby, because Mel left the nipple slip from her mouth and began to cry.

"No. Please not Maggie and Tom. Please." After burping the baby and putting her back in her crib, Tru went to the phone and called the airport, but she was told that no details were available.

Later that morning, Mrs. Diaz arrived. As she cleaned she kept glancing from Tru to the television and back again, her face creased in concern. Suddenly the doorbell rang.

When Tru opened the door and saw the uniformed

policeman and Len Doran from Tom's firm, she had to bite her lip to keep from screaming.

"They were in the front section of the plane, Tru," Len explained to her. "The plane nosed down and crashed. That's why there was so much damage in the forward cabins."

"I see." Tru faced them dry-eyed.

"Why it overshot the runway we simply don't know, but we'll be able to tell you more in the near future, miss," one of the policemen assured her.

"Thank you."

"Could I make some calls for you, Tru? I know you were closest to family Tom and Maggie had, but I thought there might be someone you'd wish to contact." Len Doran leaned forward to take her hand. "You mustn't worry about anything, you know. Tom was very thorough with his estate. You and the baby are sole beneficiaries of everything and you are the baby's guardian."

"I know. Tom told me." Tru wept then, scalding, bitter tears for the loss of her friends and for Mel who would never get to know her wonderful parents.

"I will stay with you for a few days, *señora*," Mrs. Diaz announced. "It is not good for you to be alone at a time like this."

"Thank you, Mrs. Diaz."

Telling Ellen was one of the hardest things that Tru had ever had to do and she thanked God that Randy was with Ellen when she called.

Randy took the phone from Ellen when she began to sob. "Don't worry, Tru. I'll take care of her. What can we do for you?"

"Things are working out pretty well. There's to be a small memorial service, but the two of you don't have to make the trip for that. I've had a great deal of help from people at Tom's firm and I have the baby to care for and the business to run, so I'll keep busy. Thank you anyway, Randy. Take care of Ellen."

Day by day the focus of Tru's life began to change. The divorce had gone through, and she had taken back her maiden name. She was a single woman again. But somehow none of that seemed important anymore. Mel was the only thing that mattered. Through Ellen she'd heard that Thane had been seen in the company of a cover girl. That was all right with her—it had to be. She was a mother now, and everything that had gone on before seemed to be from some other life.

Tru began to take long walks in the middle of the day so that Mel, despite the cold of New York City, could get a bit of fresh air. The business was important to her, and it was doing quite well. But nothing took precedence over Mel. And if more than once she looked at Mel and fantasized Thane as her father, Tru was able to deal with that too.

Len Doran came by once or twice a week to check on her and Tru was grateful for his kindness.

Two weeks after the accident Mrs. Diaz was evicted from her apartment, and was very upset.

"Come to us, Mrs. Diaz. I have plenty of room. You can have the suite upstairs." Tru had moved into the more spacious downstairs area to be closer to the baby. Going to sleep each night in her friends' bedroom had been hard at first, but she somehow knew they would have approved.

"Then you must call me Juana, Señora Tru, *por favor.*"

"*Sí.* I will call you Juana."

Life slowly evolved for the three of them, and if the pain of losing Thane, then her two dear friends, made the shadows deepen under Tru's eyes, and the weight melt off her frame, she ignored those things.

When she looked at her wonderful child and thought of her thriving business, she felt thankful.

One night in early December Len Doran called. "Would you have dinner with me tomorrow evening, Tru?" She knew he'd been working up to this for some time. "Don't say no. You need to get out for a little rest and recreation. You're allowed. And I know that Juana loves to take care of Mel."

"All right. Thank you, Len. I'd like to go."

"Wonderful. I'll call for you at seven."

Tru had a harder time dressing for dinner the next evening than she thought she would. She was nervous!

"Do you believe how silly your mommy is, Mel, darling? Out of whack and shaky because she's going on a date?" Tru was in the habit of keeping the baby with her whenever possible and chatting with her as though Mel could understand. Much to her amusement she began to realize that Juana was just as determined to have the baby with her.

When Mel gurgled up at her, Tru turned away from the mirror and leaned down to hug the baby who was lying in the portable crib, eyeing the mobile that swung overhead. "You're absolutely right, darling. I should have more gumption. After all, it's only a dinner date, not a trip to Tahiti." Tru faced the mirror and gave a last pat to her hair before turning to gather up the baby and kiss her cheeks. "I'll go out with Len and enjoy myself." As Tru chucked the baby under the chin Juana knocked on the door and entered.

"Ah, señora, you play with Mellie when you should be dressing," Juana scolded, shaking her head and reaching for the child. "Mr. Doran is in the living room. You go out to him and I will put our *niña* to bed."

"Thank you, Juana. Goodnight, sweetie."

"Much to her surprise Tru did have fun. The dinner, at a small out-of-the-way French restaurant in the Village, was excellent.

"I'm glad you enjoyed the food, Tru. I've always loved this place."

"No one makes sauces like the French." Tru dabbed at her mouth and sat back and sighed, smiling at Len. "Everything was wonderful."

"I think I should take you out to dinner more often. You're too thin. You have lovely bones, my dear Tru, but they show too much. You need more meat on them." Len laughed when Tru made a face at him.

"You've been talking to Juana. She's always giving me trouble about how little I eat, even though I tell her I love her cooking, which I do. Actually I think I've gained a pound or two since Juana came to live with us."

"I think you should try for five or ten."

"Heavens, I'll be eating six meals a day. Juana might strangle me." Tru smiled. "Actually I don't know what I would do without her."

"She is a wonder with the house and your little girl." Len had easily come to think of Mel as Tru's child. He had been a boon to Tru, seeing to it that Maggie and Tom's estate was administered properly.

Now he thought how really lovely Tru was as he sipped his after-dinner drink. "From what I've seen of your financial statements, you're very much in the black there too." He leaned forward, his face creased. "You don't have to work as you do, Tru. Tom's insurance could see you through if you wanted to work at a slower pace."

Tru shook her head. "No. All that money is for Mel's education and future. I have already made plans to have it invested for her."

Len nodded. "Good idea, but there will be interest

from it. No reason you couldn't use some of that for household expenses."

"I don't know, Len, I really feel that since Tom and Maggie . . ." Tru's throat suddenly felt tight. She had to cough to clear it. "If they were good enough to give me a business, then I don't need anything else. The money is for Mel."

Len shook his head, calling for the check and signing it. "Stubborn lady. Come along, Ms. Wayland, mother of one beautiful daughter, we are going to Elaine's to dance."

It shocked Tru that it was one o'clock in the morning when she finally arrived home. The evening had flown by. She'd almost forgotten how much she loved to dance.

Len said goodnight to her in the foyer of the brownstone, kissing her gently on the mouth and leaving at once.

Tru felt a pleasant warmth, nothing like the emotional maelstrom she'd experienced with Thane. Thane! Why had she thought of him now?

She looked in on the baby, changing her and then placing her on her tummy again, the way she liked to sleep. From there she went into the office and checked the answering machine, pressing the reset button and listening to the words. She wrote down everything that she would need to forward to her clients in the morning.

There was one message from Ellen, who insisted that Tru call right away, no matter how late it was when she got home. Tru laughed out loud. Ellen would never change. Everything always had to be done by yesterday.

Glancing at her watch she realized that it wouldn't be much past ten on the coast, so she dialed her friend's number.

"Tru! Where have you been? Never mind that.

Randy and I are getting married," Ellen squealed to her friend. "We're going to tie the knot on Christmas Eve. Don't tell me we're crazy. I know that."

"About time you put him out of his misery." Tru chuckled back.

"But I can't get married unless you're here as my maid of honor. I won't take no for an answer because I've already told Randy I won't marry him, ever, unless you're here."

"That's crazy." Tru laughed again, but suddenly she panicked. How could she go back to California? How could she face all the problems she left there?

"Tru," Ellen wailed. "You *can't* let me down. Say you'll come."

Tru took a deep breath. "Don't you know I wouldn't *let* you get married unless I was there to make it official."

"And will you bring your . . . daughter?" Ellen was one of the few people who knew the whole story about Mel, and that Tru was in the process of adopting the child.

It flashed through her mind that Ellen would want to see the baby who was all that was left of her dear friend, Maggie. "That might be a good idea. I'm sure your family will want to see her."

"Oh, please, bring her, Tru. There are a million people who are dying to see your little girl and scads of them will want to babysit her while you march down the aisle in front of me."

"Just a million?"

"You know what I mean. You will come and bring Mel, won't you?"

"I'll try."

"You don't have to worry about getting a flight. I've already booked a reservation for you."

"My friend, the manipulator." Tru half laughed, trying to turn back the avalanche of emotion that threatened to sweep her away. She was going home to California! Thane was there!

"Don't look so grim, chum. You can't go through life looking like you'd kill someone just because they mention Tru's name," Andy Sandilin said testily. After all, he'd only asked if Thane had been in contact with her! Andy twisted the swizzle stick in his glass, barely touching the drink in front of him. Thane was on his third Irish whiskey with a splash of water. Though Thane could hold his alcohol better than anyone Andy knew, it wasn't like him to drink that much, especially at lunch.

Now Andy regretted mentioning that Ellen had called Tru. Thane had cut him off at once, saying that he didn't want to discuss her. With that, an implacable cold shell had formed around him. Andy had never seen his friend act this way before.

"We met for lunch, chum. Not an analysis session," Thane answered acerbically, amazed at the pain he still felt at the mention of Tru's name. "I came because we haven't seen each other in a while. But I won't sit here and listen to you tell me how I should act."

"I would say that eight months is more than a while," Andy interrupted brusquely.

Thane shrugged. "Making the daily bread."

"You could buy Sacramento with what you already have socked away, so don't give me that crap," Andy confronted his glowering friend.

"Ellen didn't get an answer to the wedding invitation she and Randy sent you. She wants you there, Thane. Are you going to let her down?"

"Put like that, Andrew, it sounds like blackmail." Thane quaffed his drink and cocked his head at his friend. "Want another?"

"No. I'd rather eat."

"As you wish."

Andy worked his way through the prawn cocktail and the broiled venison they'd ordered, but he noticed that Thane ate little, though he'd always had a good appetite. His friend's color was bad, his features graven, his eyes lusterless. He'd lost weight and there were lines etched at the sides of his mouth, silver strands at his temple. What's more, Andy had all through lunch never heard Thane sound as disaffected as he had. His sense of humor had always been needle-sharp, but now it had turned sardonic and cutting. Andy had the feeling that he'd have to tell Ellen Thane wouldn't be coming to the wedding. And frankly, he was beginning to think it might be for the best.

Anyway, it certainly didn't seem the moment to mention to Thane that Tru was going to be in the wedding party . . . and that she was bringing her daughter.

"When will I see you again?" Andy said after they'd paid the check. A sadness came over him as he studied Thane.

Thane shot him an amused look. "How about Christmas Eve? At the wedding?"

"Thane." Andy grabbed his hand and pumped it. "Ellen will be delighted."

"Good. Tell her I send my love." Thane turned away abruptly and strode toward his car.

Andy opened his mouth to call him back, tell him that Tru was coming, but something stopped him.

Driving across town Thane realized how little he looked forward to Ellen's wedding, even though he was fond of her. But just the thought of seeing so many of the people who had been gathered together the night he'd met Tru made his stomach churn.

Even now as he maneuvered through the traffic to his office, he felt a jab of pain just thinking about her. "Living in New York, in partnership in an answering service company." Billy had given him a full report on Tru, but nothing had sunk in really, not after seeing her on the stoop with her arms around another man's neck, smiling into his eyes. Thane had seen that picture in his mind hundreds of times over the last months.

Finally he had decided not to contact her. Tru had made it very clear that she didn't want him in her life. "And I don't want her," Thane shouted, banging the steering wheel with his fist before he turned to go down into his building's underground garage. He would get her out of his system if it killed him. And his date tonight with Clarinda Koles, a gorgeous model and fledgling movie actress, would help.

Six

The flight to California was crowded but uneventful. Still, Tru had a feeling of trepidation she couldn't shake. There was a chance Thane would be at the wedding, but then again, maybe he'd guess she would be there and not show up himself. In fact, there was a good chance Andy would tell him that she was to be in the wedding ceremony.

Though their relationship hadn't lasted long, she felt she knew Thane. He'd have interpreted her departure as "dumping" him. He hated her now. Tru was sure of that.

Tru's thoughts were interrupted by Mel, who wanted her bottle. After being fed, the baby slept for a short time, then woke irritable and restless.

"Please let us take her and change her for you, Mrs. Wayland."

Tru looked up, startled by the two flight attendants who were reaching for Mel. They had been in the air a little over an hour. "You don't have to . . ."

"We'd love to, really. Besides so many of the other passengers would love to see this little sweetie all decked out for the holidays in her red velvet jump suit."

Tru smiled. "I couldn't resist it. It seemed like such a good outfit for traveling."

"And she looks so precious with that velvet bow in her one little curl on top of her head," crooned another one of the stewardesses.

Tru had to grin at how quickly they forgot her once they lifted the gurgling Mel up.

As they made their way along the aisle they had to stop several times so that Mel could be admired. Her daughter was a performer to be sure, Tru thought as she craned her neck to watch their progress to the galley in the mid-section of the plane.

Later, Mel slept in her seat the rest of the way, but Tru was too keyed up to close her eyes.

When the plane banked for its approach over Los Angeles International, Tru felt as though all the blood had been squeezed from her body. Outside the window sunshine gleamed off the wing. Inside Tru felt cold and tense.

She waited until the last of the passengers had gone down the aisle before gathering up the baby, the diaper bag, and overnight case she'd carried onto the plane.

One of the male attendants took Mel from her. "I'll carry her, Mrs. Wayland. Is someone meeting you?"

"Yes."

As Tru came through the mobile corridor into the main body of the terminal, she heard Ellen call out to her.

"Tru, I'm over here." Ellen waved both arms, running toward her. "Oh, Tru. Tru, you're home. I've missed you so."

Tru embraced her friend, feeling hot tears stream down her face.

•   •   •

"I think she's been permanently spoiled," Tru told Clare Sandilin, Ellen's sister-in-law, "but she seems to be thriving. I have to give a blow-by-blow report of her condition to Juana every day, and if things don't sound right to her, I'm sure she'll be on the next plane out here." Tru glanced at the large group of people gathered in the Sandilin house, where she was staying.

At the moment there was a reception going on for Randy's parents who had come in from Minnesota for the wedding.

Clare laughed. "No wonder. Your baby's beautiful, Tru. Andy and I have decided, just since Mel's arrival, that it's time to start our family." Clare shrugged at Tru's skeptical glance. "Well, actually we have been thinking about it for a while, but Mel iced it for us." She scrutinized Tru. "I wish I could say that Mel's mother looks as good as she does. Now, don't glare at me. You are too thin and you must have been working too hard to put such circles under your eyes." Clare smiled at another one of the guests who strolled past them. They were sitting together on a twin lounger next to the pool, which had been covered over in a Plexiglass dome.

"The business takes a great deal of time." Tru tried to be vague as she had no wish to discuss the sleepless nights she'd spent thinking about Thane. "I've always liked this room. Enclosing the pool with Plexiglass was such a great idea!"

"True. And wasn't it nice of them to have a reception for Randy's parents, and of course there's the wedding in two days." Clare's voice was laced with sarcasm. "I also realize that you just deliberately changed the subject . . ."

"Sorry, Clare," Tru said. "I just can't discuss . . . everything."

"I understand . . . more than you think." Clare

touched her arm gently. "But don't protect yourself too much from your friends, Tru. Whoops, my mother-in-law is signaling me to come and admire the baby again. She's so subtle." Clare kissed Tru's cheek and hurried away.

Tru leaned back in the lounger, watching the people clustered around Mel. Soon it would be time to put the baby down for a nap, but she felt so tired all at once herself. Surely it wouldn't hurt to close her eyes for a minute.

Tru had been on the run since her arrival in Los Angeles three days ago and she felt wrung out. Everyone had been so solicitous and loving to her. It had pained her, somehow, to see the concern in their eyes.

Today there had been more people to meet, most of them relatives of Randy's.

Tru opened her eyes, startled and embarrassed, wondering where Mel was and how long she'd dozed.

"Just as I came in the house your eyes were closing. You've been sleeping about five minutes." Tru looked up to see Thane Stoner. She blanched, amazed at the way he could still read her mind, even after all these months.

Tru was shocked to see how ashen and dissipated he was; he looked out of condition, dulled at the edges, not the same crisp, dynamic man who'd swept her off her feet almost a year ago. Oh, his clothes and accessories were still the same: Savile Row, Armani, Gucci, smart as they had always been. But there wasn't the same spark. "What are you doing here? Where is Mel?"

"I was invited—and that reminds me, I haven't spoken to my hostess yet, but she seems busy with someone's child. Who's Mel?" Thane's brusque words were like hurled stones. As he spoke he noticed that she looked fragile, breakable. At that moment part of him wanted to do just that . . . break her in half.

Tru swiped at her hair and swung her legs off the lounger on the side away from Thane, then stood. She took a deep breath and faced him, feeling the blood thunder in her ears. Despite the fact that he didn't look well, he was still the most beautiful man she'd ever seen. "Mel is my child." She dropped her bomb and spun on her heel, walking toward the throng around her daughter.

Thane stood there, staring at the spot where Tru had been, his body shut down for the longest thirty seconds of his life. "Son of a bitch." He spat the words, shaking with the force of his anger. Fire and ice shot through him. His breath came in painful gasps.

Finally, like an automaton, he turned slowly to watch the hubbub around Tru and the child. Thane's eyes fixed on the laughing baby as he moved toward the group. She was a beautiful little thing with Tru's blond coloring and fair skin. Would she have her mother's sapphire-blue eyes?

"Thane! Dear, look at the baby. Isn't she precious?" Cora Sandilin proffered the child happily.

Mrs. Sandilin hadn't seen Tru's protective move toward the child as Thane lifted the baby in his arms, but Thane had seen it. Thane didn't look at any of the others. Only Tru and the baby held his attention. He stared down at the now solemn infant, seeing the uncertainty there.

"Hello, beautiful baby." Thane's resonant voice broke the spell for Mel and she gurgled at him. Thane smiled back, noting that the baby's eyes were a soft sherry brown. It suddenly struck him that the baby's eyes were more like his own than Tru's. . . . His head snapped her way.

"What is it? What's wrong?" Tru felt a rising alarm. Without thinking she moved suddenly, snatching the baby from him and cradling her in her arms. She saw the surprised looks some of the others gave her from the corner of her eye, but she didn't care. Thane was a threat to her baby! A strong, instinctive maternal sense told her that.

"Easy does it, mama," Thane drawled, making the others chuckle, the tense moment evaporating.

"I . . . I should put her down for her nap now." Tru turned without another word and took Mel down the hall to the bedroom.

Mrs. Sandilin had thought of everything, even managed to obtain a portable crib for the baby. Tru was grateful to the older couple, who had always been like second parents to her. Even though they were busy with the wedding, they had insisted that she and Mel stay with them.

When Tru had argued that she should stay in a hotel, she'd been overridden by the Sandilins and Ellen. Tru had to admit that it was far easier caring for the baby when there was a kitchen just a short walk from the bedroom, and a bathroom near by.

She changed Mel and gave her a bottle and was just putting her down when she sensed that someone had come into the room. Tru straightened and whirled, her body falling unconsciously in a protective attitude in front of the crib. "You. What do you want? Leave. I'll be right out."

"I didn't come to see you. I came to see my . . . daughter."

Shock held her mute for a moment. "What? Are you crazy?" Tru reeled, staring at him, not sure if she'd heard him correctly.

"Did you think that I wouldn't notice that she has her father's eyes."

"I don't care if you noticed that or not. She *does* have her father's eyes, only . . ."

"And I'm going to see to it that she grows up with her father's name." Thane grated his teeth together.

"Now you listen to me . . . You arrogant, overbearing bastard, don't you dare try to get tough with me." Tru felt herself swung into the air, her feet leaving the ground. "What's the matter with you? What are you doing? You'll upset the baby."

"She's asleep." Thane looked down at Tru as she struggled to free herself. Suddenly all he could feel was her body against his. She was arousing him. Damn her! "How dare you hide my child from me?"

Tru sputtered, trying to free her hands so that she could strike him. "You insufferable egotist . . . Mel is not your child . . ."

"Yet you say she's yours."

"Stop interrupting me. You never let me finish a sentence. Of course she's mine and no one else's."

Thane set her on her feet again with a thud that made her hair swing about her face. "The hell she isn't. She's mine and I'm going to see to it that the world knows it. Damn you."

Tru swept her hair back from her face, planting her fists on her hips. "Damn *you*, Thane Stoner if you think that you can play games with my child . . ."

"You're the only one playing games. You're the one who's trying to put something over on me."

"You're interrupting me again." Tru knew her voice was rising, but she didn't care.

Neither noticed when the door opened.

"Hey, hey, what's going on in here? The guests have stopped talking to listen to you two battle it out in here."

Both Thane and Tru turned to glare at Andy as he stood in the doorway.

"Get out of here, Andy. We have to thrash something out." Thane's hands curled into fists.

"Sorry, old man, but my dear mother and father wanted me to intervene, so I'm afraid I'm here to stay."

"Oh, Andy, I'm sorry." Tru felt the blood run up her neck. She shot an angry look at Thane, her chin lifted. "Please leave."

"I will, but this isn't the end of it, Tru, not by a long shot." Thane sprang past his friend, anger in every line of his body.

"Whew! What was that all about, Tru?"

"Nothing, Andy. He was just doing his King Kong imitation." Tru tried to smile, but her mind was already ticking away. She would have to leave California as soon as possible. No way was she waiting until the day after New Year's, as the Sandilins had planned. The sooner she was away from Thane Stoner, the better—for both Mel and her.

The day of the wedding dawned clear and warm. Christmas had come to California bathed in glistening sunlight that blinded and delighted everyone connected with Ellen's wedding.

Though the wedding was in the afternoon the house came alive early in the morning, with Mel the center of attention over breakfast. Ellen ricocheted between ecstasy and breakdown, part of her yearning for Randy, the other part desperately wanting to make a run for the border.

"Oh, Mellie, how can you sit in your little chair chortling and kicking your legs while your auntie is going to the guillotine?"

"I don't think Randy would like that description of your wedding . . . and let me feed the baby. You're getting cereal all over both of you." Tru had to laugh

at her morose friend. It was so in character for Ellen
to have highs and lows of emotion. "Everything has
been taken care of," Tru soothed, wiping the baby's
chin, then lifting her onto her lap to give her a
bottle.

"What if Randy changes his mind?"

"Not a chance." Tru leaned over and kissed her
friend's cheek, neither of them hearing the front
door open and close.

"My goodness." Ellen straightened in her chair, looking over Tru's head. "Thane! I didn't expect you here
this morning. I hope you and Tru aren't going to
duke it out again. All the beautiful crystal that Randy
and I got for gifts is in the dining room." Ellen wore
her characteristic grin.

"Hi, brat. Nervous?"

"Thane, you heel. Why did you say taht? Eek, look at
the time. I have to shower and do my nails and all
that stuff." Ellen was up and out the door, before
Tru could call her back.

"Good morning, Tru."

"Good morning." Tru set the bottle on the kitchen
table and lifted the baby to her shoulder.

Mel burped gently, her eyelashes fluttering. She
was all ready for her morning nap.

"I've never heard a baby do that before, even though
I know they should after having a bottle," he said in
wonderment. Thane's breath lifted the hair on Tru's
neck. He saw how she flinched and his volatile temper flared again. "Don't act as though I were going
to do something antisocial. I don't like it."

Tru whirled on the chair to face him. "What did
you expect? You acted like Conan the Barbarian
yesterday and I didn't like it."

Thane glared at her.

"Excuse me." She rose to her feet. If she didn't put
Mel to bed now, she would have no time to get ready

herself. She had her fingers crossed that Mel, who had been more fussy than usual because of the strange surroundings, would nap long enough for her to shower and dress. Also, Tru had promised to do Ellen's hair.

"Excuse me. I have to change her and put her to bed for a bit and then get ready." Tru didn't even glance at Thane when she sailed out of the room with Mel in her arms.

It was when she put the baby down in the crib that she felt the prickle of awareness. Covering the baby, she straightened and turned. "Get out of here," she whispered through her teeth.

"You said you were busy," Thane said smoothly. "I won't get in your way. I'll just watch her for a short time, then leave."

Tru stood there, undecided.

"I have no intention of taking the baby while you're in the shower." Thane bared his teeth. "Which doesn't mean that I won't fight you for her in court if we don't come to an agreement. Now, go and get into the shower. I'll be leaving in a few minutes anyway."

"I don't know what you're talking about, but I do know that you shouldn't be here at all. You're not in the wedding," Tru shot at him, feeling angry that her heart was beating painfully fast just because he was near.

"I have every right to see my daughter." His face pushed forward.

"You're insane. She isn't yours, she's mine."

"Don't try to smoke me, Gertrude. It won't work again."

Tru took a step back, appalled at the wild look in his eyes. "Shh, you'll waken her," she told him.

"Take your shower," Thane commanded.

All the while she washed her body and shampooed her hair, Thane's words went round and round in her head. How could he think such a thing? Mel was hers and no one else's. Damn Thane Stoner and his autocratic jumping to conclusions!

When she warily came out of the bathroom, still rubbing her head with a towel, Mel was sleeping and Thane was gone. With a sigh of relief she put him from her mind and began to dress and make up.

Ellen was a basket of nerves an hour before the ceremony, even though she had been reassured by one and all that far from running from his bride, Randy had called her mother twice to see how Ellen was holding up.

At the crucial moment, at the back of the church, Ellen became calm and Tru felt as though *she* would fall apart.

As she preceded Ellen down the aisle, her eyes flew to where Thane stood watching her. When she passed him, he leaned forward, his motion barely discernible to those who had their eyes glued to the bride and her father coming directly behind Tru.

"I'll never let you get away from me again," Thane whispered, his lips scarcely moving.

The words thundered through Tru. She faltered, her body rocking, her eyes flying to his face, now devoid of anything but polite interest. The quick glance showed Tru that Katherine Vogt, Ellen's mother's best friend, was sitting just in front of Thane, babysitting Mel. As she watched, Thane reached out and touched the baby's tiny hand as it rested on the older woman's shoulder. Tru was sure he was sending her a message about Mel. A shudder ran through her body. It took all her willpower not to turn and snatch Mel from Thane's reach. Then she was past the pews, looking at Randy and Ellen's brother as they waited at the front of the church, both of them smiling.

The ceremony was a blur for Tru. When it was

over they all retraced their steps down the aisle, the bride and groom clinging to one another ecstatically as they greeted the wedding guests at the door.

People kissed not only the bride and groom, but Andy—Randy's best man—and Tru, as well. So many passed by that Tru was in a daze, smiling, proffering her cheek, murmuring what she hoped were suitable responses.

"Not on the cheek, darling," Thane told her just before he swept her close to him and kissed her fully on her surprised, open mouth, his hands caressing her back.

Tru pulled back, her breath coming in ragged gasps as she struggled to tell him what she thought of him.

"I thought it was wonderful too, sweetheart," Thane murmured, moving on to shake Andy's hand as Ellen's bemused brother studied them both. "Andy. Glad to see you held up so well since I'll be wanting you to perform the same duties for me soon." Thane looked back at a still agitated Tru who was trying to smile at a simpering matron while glaring at him at the same time. "You'd like Andy to be in our wedding, wouldn't you sweetheart?"

"You . . ." Tru struggled ineffectually to summon up every insulting epithet she could think of. Before she could voice them, another guest grasped her hand.

"An announcement, Thane?" Andy managed to ask in between greeting guests. He shook his head, laughing at his friend, who had stepped out of the line and was leaning against a huge gothic pillar, his hot glance lazily assessing Tru.

"I'll let Tru do the announcing." Thane pushed away from the pillar and moved on to greet the parents of the bridal pair while Tru boiled.

"Tru, are you going to marry him?" Andy asked her when the last guest had passed.

"Don't be absurd. Oh, there's Katherine and Mel. Excuse me. I must get the baby."

Before Tru could take a step Mrs. Vogt waved and shook her head. "Not to worry, Mrs. Wayland. Mr. Stoner has volunteered to take Mel and me to the reception. Bye, we'll see you there." Mrs. Vogt turned and handed the baby to Thane, who swiveled to give Tru a slow, wicked smile.

"Someday someone is going to push that man out of a jet plane. Of all the insufferable . . . nerds. He has virtually kidnapped my child," Tru sputtered.

Andy looked toward the threesome disappearing out the huge oaken doors of the church. "Nah. He'll meet us at the reception. Besides he seems smitten with Mel like the rest of us, other little sister."

"He's a cretin."

"I've heard his business rivals describe him in a similar manner." Andy chuckled as he led Tru to the car that would be following the bride and groom's limousine.

Tru was on tenterhooks all the way to the reception. Before Andy could come around to help her from the car, she leaped out and looked around the huge parking lot of the country club where the reception was being held to see if she could spot Thane's car. Her heart fell to her shoes when she couldn't find him in the crowd.

"Were you looking for us?"

Tru whirled around, feeling the muscles in her jaw relax somewhat when she spotted the baby in Thane's arms. "I'll take her." Tru reached for the baby, who gave her a big smile.

"Don't be silly." Thane barred Tru's way. "You have to be in the pictures and in the receiving line and eat at the head table." Thane's autocratic tone made her want to slug him. Instead, she bit her lip, not wanting to make a scene at Ellen's reception, seeing the sarcastic glint in his eyes and the hard thrust of his jaw.

"You go ahead, darling, I'll watch our baby," Thane told her in dulcet tones.

"Isn't that sweet?" a chubby matron effused, batting her eyes at Thane, who beamed back at her and chucked the baby under the chin. "She has your eyes." She turned and beamed at Tru. "How lucky you are to have such a husband."

"Oh, he's a regular Daddy Warbucks," Tru said through her teeth, ignoring the raised eyebrows of the matron and kissing Mel's cheek.

Thane leaned down to her. "Kiss me too, Mommy."

"Back off or I'll smack you in the mouth, wedding or no wedding," she said through clenched teeth.

"Why, sweetheart, how you talk," Thane responded sweetly. "But don't let me stop you. I'll just give the baby back to Katherine Vogt and we can go a few rounds right here in front of everyone."

"Neanderthal," Tru breathed, spinning on her heel and marching back to Andrew, her chin high.

"Whoa, other little sister, I hope that glimmer in your eyes isn't for me. The last time you looked like that I ended up face down in the mud."

"I am going to kill your best friend, Andrew."

"Oh? Don't give me any of the details. I can't stand the sight of blood." Andrew winked at her and took her arm.

The picture-taking session and receiving line were a streaky blur to Tru because she couldn't keep her mind on any of it.

The bride and groom led off the dancing after dinner. Then Andy and Tru danced, followed by the parents of the bridal couple. Finally the guests took to the floor.

When Tru was free of her bridal attendant duties, she went over to where Mel was lying in a carry cot not too far from the head table. She lifted the child, who blinked at her, yawning. "Hello, my sleepy darling. Soon I'll take you back to the house."

"No need, Tru, I'm going to take her back to the Sandilins' and put her to bed for you," Katherine told Tru. "It's all arranged. So kiss Mel good night."

Tru knew that she couldn't really leave the reception, though she longed to take Mel and grab the first plane East.

Still, it was a relief that Thane no longer had the baby, so she helped dress Mel, then walked Mrs. Vogt to the door.

Thane swept her into his arms when Tru walked back into the ballroom of the country club. "Shall we dance?"

"No," Tru told him tightly as they moved around the floor.

"Darling, relax. You're stiff as a board. I know you love to dance." Thane kissed her hair.

"Not with you."

Fury laced through him and he had to fight to control it. "Get used to it, love. I'm going to be in your life from now on. You can marry me or we'll live together. Either way Mel will have my name and will be my heir, that is, unless we have more children."

"Stop it. I am not marrying you."

"Fine. Then we'll live together."

"And I'm not living with you either. I am getting back on that plane in two days and returning to New York."

"I can live in New York. Much of our business is in the East and we have an office in the Stoner-Wilde Building."

Tru stared up at him, wanting to smack the smile off his face. Damn him! He owned a skyscraper in

Manhattan. It took all her control not to kick him in the shins. "I have a business to run and—"

"So do I."

Tru seethed. "Don't interrupt me."

"Darling, your face is red. Shall I get you a cool drink?"

"I want nothing from you. Ah. Don't do that." Tru gasped when Thane bent her over in a dip, brought her up again, then whirled her away from his body and back again, making her dizzy.

"I like New York." Thane held her close, feeling the quiver run through her body. Dammit! Why did she fight him on everything?

"My life is set now."

"So is mine, but I'm flexible. I understand from Ellen that you live in a brownstone. That should be comfortable for both of us."

"No."

"As you wish. We'll look for an apartment. The East Seventies are nice. What do you think?"

"No."

"All right. Then how about Connecticut? We could commute."

"I mean no, I don't want you in my house." Tru stopped dancing, taking a step backward. She had never seen his eyes shine so bright, his mouth set so firmly.

Thane placed his hands at her waist, slowly tightening his grip, lifting her onto her tiptoes. "I'm in your life, lady, anyway it takes, until the time that Mel is on her own, away at college."

"College?" Tru moaned faintly.

Thane stared down at her testily. "Of course. I want my daughter to go to Harvard."

"Harvard?"

"Stop repeating everything I say, like some damned parrot."

Tru rallied from the fog that seemed to hold her. "Don't you call me names, buster, or I'll kick you in the knee."

Both of them were so caught up that they were unaware of others around them. Neither saw Mrs. Sandilin's approach.

"Children, for heaven's sake, you're turning heads." Mrs. Sandilin came up to them, her mouth twitching when they both rounded on her, glowering. "I certainly hope that Mel isn't going to grow up as cross as you two have been lately."

"He is not her father."

"She certainly won't."

Thane and Tru answered at the same time.

Mrs. Sandilin laughed out loud. "You both have the same frown on your faces." She kissed each one on the cheek. "Now behave yourselves. The bride and groom will be leaving soon."

When the older woman walked away Tru looked back at Thane. "I did not want to have this discussion with you here."

Thane cocked his head in a mocking salute. "Choose the time. I'll be ready."

Tru walked away from him, her mind churning with the idea of Thane coming to New York and living in the brownstone. It was bizarre and appalling . . . yet wildly appealing. Tru felt pulled apart by the conflicting emotions rioting in her.

She wanted Thane, but she dreaded being with him. Her life had begun to take shape without him and she didn't want to be thrust back into the purgatory she'd gone through when she'd first lived in New York. Climbing out of the pit had been perhaps the hardest thing she'd ever had to do, but she had learned from it. And the mere thought of bleeding to death all over again, if she and Thane chose to live together and then they parted once more, was too much to contemplate. No! Mel and her mama would return to New York alone. They would find a way to be happy without him. With Mel and the business, life would be complete enough.

"Tru! Where are you going? They're going to take more pictures," Clare called to her.

"What? All right, I'll be right there. Just going to freshen up."

Once in the ladies' room Tru pressed wet towels to her face in an effort to calm herself. After that she applied more blusher and lip gloss, spraying her wrists with a subtle, cooling perfume.

Feeling at last more in control, she went out for the pictures and then helped Ellen don her going-away clothes.

When Ellen insisted that all the single women guests line up for the throwing of the bouquet, Tru wanted to make herself disappear, but the Sandilins insisted she take part.

Tru found an inconspicuous corner to stand in under the winding staircase where Ellen would position herself when she threw her bouquet. It was the best spot she could think of to avoid the flowers. Marriage was certainly not in the cards for her.

Suddenly the bouquet came sailing through the air. Tru put her hands up instinctively to block the flowers, but instead, they settled right into her grasp. "Good Lord," she said, then moaned. She should never have underestimated the determination of Ellen.

Thane came up to her side, smiling. He leaned down and gave her a big kiss to the thunderous applause of the onlookers. Ignoring Tru's struggles to free herself, he lifted his head and looked at their smiling audience. "Thank you for the applause. Tru and I feel this is a good omen since we will be marrying in the not too distant future."

"Stop that." Tru's protests were drowned in the roar of approval. She couldn't help but notice that Ellen and Randy were leading the clapping.

"Darling, don't make a fuss. You'll ruin Ellen and Randy's exit."

Tru was still, forcing a smile to her face when the guests, who were shooting rice at Ellen and Randy, began to pelt them with some of it too.

After Ellen and Randy had gone, the Sandilins came up to them.

"We just wanted you to know how happy we are for you, Tru, dear. We know you and Thane will have a wonderful life."

"Thank you, Mrs. Sandilin," Tru managed faintly.

Others came up to congratulate them, embracing them and shaking their hands.

"Tru, you devious creature, you never said a word when we had that long talk at the reception for Randy's parents." Clare gave her a sly smile. "I think you at least might have given Ellen a hint."

Tru couldn't seem to make her slack jaw tighten up so that she could tell them how wrong they were—she had no intention of marrying Thane Stoner.

"She can be secretive." Thane slipped his arm around Tru's waist, his grip tightening when she tried to pull away.

Andrew looked from one to the other, scrutinizing Tru the longest. "When is the wedding?" He grinned when she shot him a scathing glance.

"Soon. But not before we go back to New York," Thane answered easily.

"We?"

Clare and Tru spoke at the same time.

Thane looked down at Tru, feeling a macabre satisfaction that she was his captive, that he'd caught her off balance. Thane knew full well she was doing her level best to keep him at a distance, that she had no plans for him to join her in New York. And knowing that she felt that way infuriated him. If he would have, he would have locked her away in a tower like Rapunzel. He felt a crazy, swelling need to dominate, to manacle, to keep. She angered and frustrated him, but he had no intention of letting her go. Life without her had been a desert. Even if they fought every day, it would be preferable to the emptiness he'd known without her in his life.

Seeing her in New York kissing another man had been like being nailed into a coffin. Only in the past month or so had he been able to function normally again. If she hadn't come to Ellen's wedding, he would have gone to New York and faced her, even though it would have meant putting every shred of pride that he had left aside.

But now Gertrude Wayland, soon to be Stoner, had performed her last escape. Once she was his wife, he'd make sure she never got the urge to leave him again. He'd also do everything in his power to make the black shadows under her eyes disappear.

Mrs. Sandilin and her husband strolled back to the group after bidding some friends good-bye, both of them beaming. "Tru, dear, we have had the most wonderful idea." The older woman looked past Tru to Thane. "Well, I can't say that it was ours alone. Actually, Thane mentioned it first . . ."

"I'm not sure I follow you." Tru spoke warily, all too aware of the strong hand that held her fast.

"We're going away, and that means you will have the house to yourself for the last two days of your stay. According to Thane, you work long hours in New York and you could use some rest."

"Thane's never seen me work in New York," Tru muttered.

"What did you say, dear? Oh, no matter, John and I have decided to go back to Las Vegas with

Katherine right after Christmas." She kissed Tru's cheek. "With Martha in the house all you'll have to do is sit around the pool, get a tan, nap or swim." Mrs. Sandilin frowned for a moment. "And it wouldn't hurt for you to have some of Martha's cooking either."

"But, Mrs. Sandilin, I don't want to chase you out of your house at holiday time."

"Don't be ridiculous, child. It will be nice for us to get away. Katherine has been after us to visit her for ages, and we do love Las Vegas. Besides, a real vacation is just what you need. Since you aren't expected back until Friday evening, you'll have two full days to relax."

"And you needn't worry about your plane reservation." Thane noted the suspicious look in her eyes when Tru whirled to face him.

"What do you mean?"

"I mean that you can cancel it. I'll be flying you back East on our company jet."

Tru heard the muffled laughter of the others only through the roaring in her ears. "No need for you to trouble yourself at such a busy time of year, Thane," she said through her teeth. "I intend to fly on my reservation. Besides, private flying could be dangerous now, what with storms and the crowded air lanes." She hurried her words.

"Darling, you must trust me to take care of you and Mel. I'm a very good pilot." Thane smiled, but he felt like smacking her.

"I don't want to change my reservation," Tru mumbled.

"Well, we'll talk about it later, darling."

Tru stared at him, mesmerized by the controlled sound of his voice and steely glint in his eyes—signs that he was in a flaming temper.

Thankfully, at that moment Mr. and Mrs. Sandilin

were called away to say good-bye to other friends, and Andrew and Tru were constrained to accompany them.

As the reception wound down Tru began to feel that her face would fall off if she smiled much longer. All she really wanted to do was run from Thane Stoner, as far away and as fast as possible.

Finally it was over. Tru gathered her things, her face aching, her body fatigued. She said good-bye to the Sandilins and went looking for Andrew, assuming she would find him in the parking lot. It would be good to get back, look in on Mel and go to bed. Tomorrow morning would be soon enough to tackle the giant problem of Thane Stoner.

"Not that way. Andrew and Clare have gone. You're coming with me." Thane gripped her arm above the elbow, steering her toward the Ferrari.

"Ouch. That hurts." Tru was almost running.

"Then stop pulling away from me. You've been doing that all damn day and I don't like it." Thane almost threw her into the passenger seat of his automobile.

Tru glared at him when he got behind the wheel, rubbing her upper arm. "I don't like being manhandled."

Thane's teeth came together with a click. "You wouldn't be if you weren't trying all your little tricks." He shot her a hard look. "If it comes to that, I'm not too charmed by the way you've been treating me either."

"Tricks? Me? How about you? Announcing to the world that we're getting married! What a farce!"

"We are getting married, Gertrude."

"My name is Tru."

"And soon it will be Tru Stoner. I won't have my daughter brought up by a single parent when she could have the stability of a two-parent home."

"For the last time, she is not your child."

"I don't like lies."

"Neither do I."

Thane whirled in his seat to face her, one hand on the back of her seat. "Tru, get this through your head. I am coming back to Manhattan with you. We are going to live together, as man and wife, I hope, but if not, then in sin. So don't try anything. I won't be so patient next time."

"You? Patient? Hah!"

"Stop being childish." Thane started the car. With a screech of tires they roared out of the parking lot.

"And do you intend to give me whiplash?"

"Don't sulk."

"I . . . am not . . . sulking." Tru gripped the dashboard to brace herself as the car shot down the avenue leading to the freeway. She had to hold herself tightly in check to keep from screaming at him. Thane Stoner was the most annoying man in the world!

Thane threw her a quick glance, his eyes noting the slight tremor in her cheek. He slowed the car. "Look, Tru, we aren't getting anywhere this way. Why don't you just relax and accept the inevitable?" He reached over and grasped her clasped hands. "I'm not going to hurt you or Mel. I love my daughter and I want you very badly . . . still."

"Thane, why do you insist on refusing to see things the way they are? Mel is not—"

"We agreed to table that discussion for a while. Let's take it one step at a time."

"Thane, it's so complicated." Was she already beginning to cave in? Would she never be able to suppress her love for him? But love was no panacea. She had discovered that the hard way, before she'd left California for New York.

"Truce? Just for now?" he asked, a winning smile on his face.

Tru nodded; she didn't feel as though she was able to trust her own voice. Thane! Back in her life! She was plummeting toward him now, and though she knew she should put the brakes on, somehow she didn't want to fight it.

"I've told Mr. and Mrs. Sandilin that I want to move into their house with you while they're gone and they've given their permission."

Tru turned in her seat, facing him, opening her mouth to speak.

Thane put his index finger on her lips. "Let me finish. I have no intention of hurrying you. I'll sleep in a separate bedroom. I just want to spend as much time as possible with you and Mel."

"Oh, Thane," she said at last, "this can't work—there are too many problems."

Thane shrugged. "Most relationships have them."

Tru cleared her throat. "I don't need this. It could all just fly apart like a bad watch at the first hint of trouble." Thane eased around a slower vehicle and shot down the freeway.

"You see me as the type who would cut and run?" His words were laced with sarcasm.

"No."

"Good. I don't see you that way either, even though you've been known to run away from things in the past." Thane lifted her hand, his tongue tracing the lines on her palm.

"Thane. Don't."

"Why? I've missed you, dammit."

His fury suddenly made her laugh. "You sound like a little boy."

"Then, you should be ashamed of yourself. You're the only person in the world who has that effect on me."

When they reached the Sandilin home, it was a beehive of activity.

Cora Sandilin met them as they entered, her cheeks pink, her eyes shining. "Oh, there you are. We've been playing with Mel. She is such a dear, Tru. I insist that you bring her home to us at least twice a year. My husband is spilling over with baby talk."

"I will bring her back again. I promise."

"And I'll make sure she does. My parents have heard about Mel and want to see her too, so we'll be visiting with them before we fly East."

Tru gasped.

"Wonderful idea." Mrs. Sandilin turned her head as someone called her name. "I'm coming, Katherine. Excuse me, children." She sailed down a hallway.

Tru looked up at Thane and said shakily, "Your parents?"

He nodded, kissing her forehead. "Yes. Not to mention the rest of the family."

"Oh, Thane, what in the world could you be thinking of? I keep telling you, Mel is *not*—"

"We'll discuss that later. Look, darling, I promise you won't feel intimidated by mother and father. I won't let that happen."

Tru could do nothing more than close her eyes and shake her head. She couldn't fight this man. He was just too strong for her.

"It will be fine, you'll see," Thane reassured her.

Christmas Eve was warm and wonderful. The baby stayed up later than usual, enthralled by the Christmas lights and the scads of toys that were opened for her.

"I didn't know she would be getting all this," Tru murmured to Mrs. Sandilin, who turned a bright red.

"It's silly I know, but it's been so long since we had a baby in this house that John and I went a little overboard."

Thane came over after dinner, saying that he'd eaten with his parents and gone to church.

When the others drifted off to bed, Thane held Tru back. "I have something for you."

"But I haven't got anything for you."

"Wrong. You and Mel are my gift." Thane lifted her left hand, taking a ring from his pocket at the same time. He slipped the emerald-cut diamond on her finger, then placed his lips there. "Now it's official, Tru. We're engaged."

Seven

Thane came over for Christmas brunch the next day.

"Cora says they'll be leaving today for Katherine's. I told her that you would be fine because I was going to take you to my parents'." He growled down at her. "Where's your ring?"

Tru lifted her hand and looked at it stupidly. "Oh. I took it off when I showered and forgot to put it back on. It's in my travel case. Thane, about me wearing a ring . . ."

"I want you to wear that ring. Now, where is Mel?" Thane strode away from her, his back stiff.

Tru stared after him, sighing.

Later, when the Sandilins and Katherine Vogt left, the house became strangely quiet. Mel was napping. Tru didn't know where Thane had gone, but she'd heard his car revving in the drive. Maybe he wouldn't come back. But as she tidied the kitchen and then tried to concentrate on a book, loneliness seized her. And Thane's face kept appearing before her. She had to admit she didn't really want to live without him.

"Hi."

Tru whirled around, spotting Thane, his stance wary, his face closed to her. "I . . . I thought you weren't coming back." Without thinking she sped across the patio, catapulting herself into his arms, great gulping sobs escaping her when he enfolded her. Shuddering sighs replaced her tears as he pressed urgent kisses to her hair and over her face.

"I'm sorry." Thane could feel her vulnerability, and it shocked him. How many times in the last year had he pictured her with her head thrown back laughing wildly as she told and retold the tale about the foolish man in California who'd tried to hold her? That had been how he'd imagined her.

When Ellen had told him of Maggie's death, he had commiserated with her, but he had been so frozen in his own misery that he hadn't put together the fact that Tru had been living with the Masons. Nor had Billy investigated long enough to learn that.

Now, though, he knew he'd been wrong about Tru all along. She'd missed him, even if she wouldn't admit it, and had been desperately lonely. How difficult it must have been to be alone in a city like New York, not only fending for herself but taking care of the baby! Pain sliced through him as he pictured it, making him tighten his grip on her. "I should have been with you, taking care of you." The words were muttered more to himself than to her.

All the while he held her, an inner voice told Tru that she should be strong—stiffen her spine, pull away, lift her chin and be independent—but the warning faded into nothingness in Thane's presence. He warmed her, gave her courage, made all the sweet things of life that she had buried come alive. With a certainty that brought desperation she knew that the myriad doubts she had about Thane would rise again, perhaps even swamp her. But right now all she knew was that she needed this man.

"Darling?" Thane felt her body quake again as he shifted so that he could study her face. "What is it? Are you coming down with something?" For a second he was taken aback at the naked want in her eyes. Then he murmured, "Tru, darling." He lifted her off the ground so that she was face to face with him, her feet dangling. "Don't hide from me. I want you badly, love. And I can read the message in your eyes." He strode to a lounge chair and sat down with Tru in his lap, cradling her there. His lips were tentative on her skin, barely grazing the surface. "You have the softest skin in the world. I love kissing you."

The world was spinning behind her closed eyelids as she felt Thane's mouth on her body, the blood spilling through her veins in a torrent as she reacted to him in the old, familiar way. It was an ecstatic, tearing agony to accept that, now, she was really and truly home in California because she was in Thane's arms.

Thane pulled back from her, his breath rasping from his throat, stunned by the speed with which she'd been able to arouse him.

He had not been celibate in the year he'd been separated from Tru. In fact, he'd done everything he could to forget her with other women, but his efforts hadn't worked. None of them were like Tru. "I'm going to make love to you. If you don't want me to, please say so now." He knew that once he started to caress her, he could never stop.

"Thane." Tru shuddered as she breathed his name. "I want you to love me . . . and I want to love you back."

Thane laughed shakily. "That's clear enough." He placed her on her back, staring down at her, his body hard and eager to possess her, to please and delight her, his mind straining with the rest of him to make her his. He steeled himself to be patient, to go slowly with her.

"Just looking at you turns me on, lady." He put his hand on her breast, kneading the yielding flesh gently, his eyes studying her every nuance of reaction. "Give yourself to me, Tru," he murmured as he lowered his mouth to the soft column of her throat, then lifted his head to watch her once more.

"Shouldn't we go into the house?" Tru felt dizzy and out of breath. Trembling with want she gripped his shoulders. It had been so long!

"Why, darling? We can hear Mel from here."

"Neighbors?"

He stroked down toward her abdomen, his fingers tugging at the material that hid her from him. Desire choked him at the first glimpse of her lush white breasts and the pink, pebble-hard nipples exposed when he unbuttoned her dress and pushed the fabric aside.

"That fence is pretty high, love," he told her absently, his gaze and hands never leaving the satin skin of her body. "And I can't even see the neighbors' rooftops from here." Thane leaned down and nuzzled the elastic top of her bikini panties with his mouth, his tongue moving upward slowly to finally caress the soft sweet mounds of her breasts. "We'll go inside in a minute."

"All right." Tru's limbs felt like lead, yet at the same time she felt as if she were floating on air. It was fantasy, yet it was also real! Thane was here! The love she'd tried to bury rose in her like a tidal wave. She draped her arms around his neck, her eyelids lifting heavily so that she could watch him. "Thane," she murmured happily, her fingers running over his face, reading it like braille, as if to reaffirm that he was really with her. "I can't believe we're doing this." Tru stopped herself before she confessed that she'd dreamed so many nights of being held in his arms, that many mornings she'd woken with tears streaming down her face, hugging herself while shudders wracked her body. Denying herself Thane's love had made her physically ill. She let her hands slide down his body, exploring tenderly, touching, pressing, rubbing, reacquainting herself with him.

All at once Tru realized that Thane was still, that he was letting her love him. It gave her great pleasure to do so. When his body seemed ready to explode with sensation, he could hold out no longer. He'd gone beyond passion into exultation; there could be no other love for him now besides Tru. He clasped her to him and pulled her onto his chest. "You're a darling."

"So are you."

Thane laughed huskily. "Crazy lady."

"I feel a little mad," Tru said.

"Tru, my angel, I want no clothes between us." Thane rolled to one side and stripped off his shirt and pants, then as quickly divested her of her bikini panties.

All thought of going into the house and the bedroom left their minds as the power between them built. Even their minds melted into a mesh of sensuous, physical response as the passion that had been with them from the first, reasserted itself.

Thane took hold of her waist, rubbing her skin against his. "I want this all the time, sweetheart."

Tru felt the touch of that urgent spear and she slid downward so that they could be joined.

"Not yet, love." Then Thane used his tongue, entering her in the most elemental way. She felt as though she'd received an electric shock. Paralyzing excitement shook her body. She gripped Thane, her hands on his shoulders pulling him upward.

"Darling! Wait. I want to love you more."

"I can't wait, Thane."

"Oh love, you set me on fire."

In gentle frenzy they joined, the rhythm of the ages drawing them on, their bodies and minds exploding in the passion that had always been theirs.

Then, bodies moist with love dew, they descended from the elevated plateau to which their love had taken them.

Thane turned his head, kissing her forehead as he held her to him. "Only you can do that to me."

"Me too," Tru said, giddily, feeling the smile quiver on her face. "I feel so—"

An unmistakable wail interrupted them.

"Uh-oh, that's Mel."

"Her timing isn't all that bad." Thane rolled off the lounger, grinning down at Tru as he reached for his cotton slacks. "Let me get her. If she acts the least bit frightened, I won't pick her up," Thane assured Tru. Then he was loping across the patio and in through the sliding door before she could say another word.

Tru scrambled for her sun dress, fumbling into it, waiting to hear Mel's indignant howl.

As she crossed the patio Thane appeared in the doorway, a rueful smile on his face, holding the baby, who was looking up at the man all agog, but not unhappily. "She's wet, Tru. Where are her things?" His worried look went from Tru to Mel. "I'm not sure I know how to change her."

Tru laughed. "I'll do it. Hi, sweetie. Have a good nap?" Tru took the baby and hugged her. Mel gurgled. "She wasn't afraid of you?"

"No, I think she was just glad to get out of her crib."

After the baby was changed and dressed in a cotton sun suit, Thane sat with her in the middle of the room, gooing to her, the baby watching him wide-eyed.

To Tru's surprise Thane didn't seem to tire of playing with the baby and when it was time to feed her, he offered to give the baby her bottle.

Tru shook her head, instinctively reluctant to give that chore to him, balking at handing over any more of her life to him than she had already. She was aware that Thane hadn't taken his eyes off her since she'd removed the baby from him, cradled Mel in her arms and fed her.

"Ah, Tru, we're expected at my folks' this evening. I promised them that I'd bring you."

"Thane, I can't. I don't have a baby-sitter." He was going too fast! Then a horrible thought struck her. "I hope you didn't tell them that the baby was yours." Tru held her breath as she waited for his answer, forcing herself to look in those agate-hard eyes.

"No, but they'll see what I saw in her eyes," Thane told her, silky menace in his voice.

Trying to keep herself on an even keel, she concentrated on Mel. Tru set the bottle on a nearby table, burped the baby, then placed her in her playpen on her stomach, in a shady part of the patio. "Thane, most people can see resemblances in any baby if they choose. That doesn't mean the baby is theirs. And Mel is not your daughter."

"Don't belabor the point. I'm getting sick of it."

"Then don't bring it up," Tru snapped at him.

The air crackled between them as they faced each other like boxers in a ring.

"And you know damn well you don't need a baby-sitter because we'll be taking Mel with us." Thane shot her an angry glance.

Turning, she stalked into the house to don her swimsuit. She couldn't be in his company an hour without arguing with him . . . even though they'd just made love.

Thane borrowed some riviera briefs from the cabana and joined her in the water, but neither said anything.

By the time the afternoon waned, Tru felt as though her nerves were stretched to the breaking point. Though she rarely looked his way she felt his stare like sunburn on her neck. At any moment she expected Thane to leave.

Later, when she was dressing Mel so that they could go and visit the Stoners, Tru noticed how her hand shook as she buttoned Mel's dress. "We are not going to the guillotine, Mellie."

The baby gurgled.

Tru couldn't seem to choose an outfit for herself after she'd dressed the baby. Her shoes fell from her hand. The only summer-weight suit she'd brought didn't seem right. All the promises she'd made herself about buying a new wardrobe once she'd settled in New York had gone out the window when Mel became her charge. Now she was frugal with her money, only buying things for the baby.

"Oh well, linen is always good and I can wear turquoise." Tru shrugged at her image in the mirror, not sure whether her upswept blond hairdo was too austere. "Too late to change." She smiled weakly at the chortling baby, who was lying on the bed staring at a sunbeam on the ceiling. "Up the rebels, Mel."

As Tru bent to lift the child there was a sharp knock at the bedroom door before it was flung open to slam against the wall.

"Close your mouth, you'll catch flies. You were taking so long I figured you'd done one of your escape acts."

Tru glared at him, straightening with the baby in her arms. "I don't have an escape act. And kindly don't come storming into my room again."

"I have no reason to trust that you'll stay put."

"And I'm not your puppet," Tru shot back.

Mel whimpered and the two adults stared at her, then glanced at each other.

In tacit agreement they quieted down and left the room.

Thane glared down at Tru before hoisting the baby into his arms while she locked the front door.

"Where did you get that?" Tru stared at the plushly outfitted infant seat in the back seat of the Rolls Royce he was driving.

"I bought it." Thane buckled the baby in, drawing her attention to the mobile he'd fastened to the ceiling.

In silence the two adults settled in the front seat, conversation sparse between them.

"Dear heaven," Tru whispered when she saw the mammoth home situated above the rolling Pacific.

"What did you say?"

"It ain't much, but it's home," Tru muttered.

"Very funny." Thane parked the car at the top of the hill in the turnaround in front of the door. Then he got out and opened the back door to get Mel.

Tru opened her own door and watched as Thane lifted the child.

"Ah, here you are. We've been waiting."

Tru spun around at the sound of the soft voice, facing the white-haired woman in the doorway, a tall, older replica of Thane standing behind her.

Tru went to the baby whom Thane was holding

and took her from him, cradling the child and trying to smile at the two older people.

"Do come in, my dear. Oh what a lovely child. Isn't she a beautiful baby, Cranston?"

"Indeed she is and so is her mother. How do you do, my dear. I'm Cranston Stoner and this is my wife, Lydia. Welcome to our home."

"Mother and Dad, this is Tru Wayland and her baby, Mel," Thane told his parents, his hand at Tru's back as though to usher her into the house . . . or keep her captive. He gave Tru a hard grin. "I'm sure she'd like you to call her Tru. Wouldn't you, darling?"

"Yes." Tru's eyes slid away from his. What was Thane trying to foment here?

"May I hold your little girl, Tru?" Mrs. Stoner turned when they entered the huge sun room off the back of the house, the three glassed-in walls giving an illusion of being outdoors. Tru could see a swimming pool and tennis court in walking distance.

"Sometimes she's a little shy with strangers." Tru handed her baby to the eager woman.

Mel immediately made a liar out of her mother by smiling and blowing bubbles at Thane's mother, her little hands patty caking the air, making both of Thane's parents beam.

"See? All the Stoners have charm," Thane whispered to Tru, his mouth at her temple.

"Not all," Tru shot back tartly.

"Darling, careful. You'll hurt my feelings."

His silky chuckle put goose bumps up her spine as his fingers casually massaged her buttocks.

Tru couldn't quite control her jerky move away from Thane. He should be caged as a public nuisance, she fumed, stationing herself closer to the older couple, who had sat down on an overstuffed couch with the baby between them.

Lydia Stoner looked at up Tru, smiling. "She is very beautiful, Tru." The older woman looked from Tru to Thane. "And we're so glad you returned to California. Thane has told us so much about you . . . and Mel." Lydia reached up one hand and clasped Tru's. "We couldn't be happier about you and Thane."

"You couldn't?" Tru's hand lay flaccid in the other woman's grip. Damn Thane! What had he told his parents?

Thane slipped his arm around Tru's waist. "Tru and I haven't told anyone but you and Dad, since we're not sure when the wedding will be."

Tru coughed to clear her throat.

Mrs. Stoner patted Tru's hand. "I understand. I just wanted you to know how thrilled we are," she went on before turning back to the gurgling child.

Tru moaned almost inaudibly.

"Don't you feel better knowing that my parents are with us?" Thane watched as her head swiveled toward him, admiring the fiery sparkle in her eyes, the slender column of her neck. Her hair had a burnished white-gold look to it, twisted on her head that way. Thane liked it.

"Will you listen to me?" Tru spoke through her teeth, one eye on the doting couple playing with the baby, the other pinned on Thane.

"Darling, I always listen to you."

"Peachy."

"Your little girl talk is cute. I guess Mel will sound like that in a year or so." Thane leaned down as she opened her mouth to continue and kissed her, his lips lingering, tasting, savoring. Even with the blood hammering in his veins he was aware of how she stiffened in his arms. Damn her! "You have a wonderful mouth, darling." His low words were like an added caress.

"Stop that. Your parents." Tru cocked her head

sideways, catching the knowing glance that passed between Lydia and Cranston Stoner.

"Don't worry, dear. We're a demonstrative family," Lydia Stoner told her kindly.

"Oh." Tru tried to get her hands up in front of her so that she could push against Thane's chest but his hold prevented any maneuvering.

Just then a white-coated servant came into the room and announced dinner.

"Julio, this is Ms. Wayland and her baby Mel." Mr. Stoner rose to his feet. Then he spoke in rapid Spanish. He turned back to Tru. "Julio and his aunt and uncle have been with our family for many years. While we eat they will take care of the baby, if that's all right with you, my dear. Otherwise, we can have a crib put in the dining room."

The interruption gave Tru a chance to break free of Thane. For a moment she scrutinized the young man, then glanced at her daughter. "Why don't we let Mel decide?" Tru suggested to Julio in hesistant Spanish.

Julio came forward and bent over the baby, who reached up a chubby fist to grasp his face.

"I think she looks comfortable," Tru smiled down at her child, then stepped back. "Oh, I'd better get her diaper bag."

"Not to worry, señora. It is all ready with my tía."

Despite Tru's trepidation dinner was not the ordeal she had pictured it being. Both older Stoners went to great lengths to put her at ease and Tru soon was able to converse with them easily.

Thane watched his parents with Tru, pleased at the warmth that flowed between them. Still, it wouldn't have mattered to him if his parents had hated Tru. He would have married her anyway. And there was no way he was going to let himself be separated from her now. If the past year taught him anything, it was that he'd rather battle with Tru for the next fifty years of his life than face the same amount of the time without her. He wanted to be in her clutches, tied to her, never freed. Accepting that had cost him a great deal, but now that he had there was no going back . . . and he wasn't about to let her be free of him.

Tru was well aware of Thane's scrutiny all through dinner as she fielded the discreet questions his parents asked her. "Yes, the answering service is demanding, but at the same time I work at home and can be with the baby. It works out very well that way."

Mrs. Stoner's eyebrows raised. "But I thought you were in California to stay, Tru."

"Oh no, Mel and I will be going home tomorrow . . ."

"And I will be going with them, Mother. I've already made arrangements to move my office there. I thought Father might have told you."

"He didn't." Lydia shot a tight-lipped look at her husband, who shrugged.

"I didn't know about this either," Tru said slowly.

Thane leaned back in his chair, his fingers caressing the handle of his fork. "Darling, I told you that we wouldn't be separated."

Tru opened her mouth to respond but no words came. Thane's bourbon-colored eyes turned bronze with menace. "I thought you might come to New York at a later time . . . to visit us," her voice trailed away lamely, her eyes sliding away from his.

"That isn't the way it's going to be," Thane announced.

"I see." His mother studied him, vaguely aware that there was a battle of wills being waged at her dinner table.

"I thought you might, Lydia, my dear." Cranston Stoner met his son's angry look with a bland smile.

By the time the liqueurs were passed around, Tru's nerves had unraveled as completely as a poorly knit sweater.

Thane was irritated that Tru had side-stepped all questions about their life together. He churned with a desire to tell her that he wasn't going to put up with her childish evasiveness.

They didn't stay too long after eating. "Mel will need a good night's sleep for tomorrow. Our flight's in the afternoon, which means we'll be arriving in New York rather late."

"I understand, my dear. Hopefully you'll come again."

"And you must visit us in New York."

"Oh they will, darling. All of us." Thane's clipped tones telegraphed his irritation. He scooped the baby from her, holding the baby bag as well, and motioned Tru out the door.

On the drive home the baby's eyes fluttered between sleeping and waking.

"She's a very good traveler, isn't she?"

Tru turned to look at Thane. "Yes, she is."

"You love her very much."

"She's my life."

Thane felt a jolt of pain so severe that he caught his breath. "You have another life, too, Tru, and please don't say it's the answering service," Thane told her harshly.

"I wasn't going to." She took a deep breath. "Thane, I think it would be a good idea if Mel and I returned to New York alone." She held up her hand when he opened his mouth. "Let me finish. There's a great deal at stake here, and I don't want Mel caught between two people who are constantly at odds. With a little time and space between us we could look at the situation more sensibly."

Tru didn't feel sensible, though. She felt sick because she was telling Thane not to come with her when she really wanted to have him with her in New York. "In that way we would have a chance to be apart and see if we both felt . . ." Her voice faltered when his head spun her way, his features contorted, his eyes slits of fury. "I only thought—"

Suddenly he banged his fist into the dash. "I know what you thought, but you can forget it. Your nasty little blueprints for our life don't bear any resemblance to reality."

"Nasty! I wasn't being nasty. I was being practical. And you stop driving like a maniac with my daughter in the car." Tru bit her lip to still its trembling.

Mel's light breathing was the only sound in the car for the rest of the journey.

As soon as she and Mel were in the house and the baby changed and placed in her crib, Thane faced her. "I'll be here tomorrow around noon. We'll get your things together, then go to the airport." Turning on his heel he stalked out the door without another word.

"Barbarian." Tru fumed, following him to the door, then watching as the Rolls Royce roared down the driveway to the road.

Tru had a troubled night. She dreamed of Thane making love to her, of the two of them writhing on the bed, dampened skin quivering in passion and want. More than once she shot to a sitting position, tangled in the sheets, perspiration coating her body, her breathing ragged, her hands flailing the air as though doing battle with something, or someone.

The next day she woke woolly-headed and out of sorts after only a couple of hours of sleep. As though sensing her mood, Mel was fractious, demanding her breakfast and brooking no hesitation on Tru's part to get it to her.

Later, Tru put the baby out on the patio in a net-covered playpen, she packed their things and placed them near the front door. She was just bringing out the last bag when the doorbell rang. Glancing at her watch as she turned the knob, she noted that it couldn't be Thane since it was only a little after ten.

"Hello, Tru. You look thin." Roger looked her up and down.

Without answering Tru tried to shut the door again, but Roger put his weight against it and forced it open. Then he walked in, his face hard and triumphant.

"None of your tricks, Tru. I don't like it."

"Get out of here."

"Not until I've said what I came to say." Marching past her he went into the Sandilins' living room. "This is nice." He looked around avidly. "Heidi and I will have a house like this one day."

"Goody. Now get out of here."

Roger whirled, glaring at her. "Sit down and listen."

"I'll stand. I can watch you better that way."

"Still the same smart aleck, aren't you? Well, it doesn't matter anyway." Roger went over to a table and picked up a vase, looking at the bottom. "Very nice."

"Get on with it."

"All right." Roger watched her. "Your friend Ellen bragged to me that you were coming back to be in her wedding . . . and that you had a baby."

"'Then she must have told you that the baby was Maggie's."

"I don't buy that. I think you got pregnant by Stoner, then went to New York to have the baby. He didn't know, did he? You made a fool out of him with his own kid. Frankly, I don't think he'd like to have something like that get out."

Tru's skin crawled with distaste at the thought of ever having been married to this man. "Didn't you try this stuff once before and get burned, Roger? Don't you ever learn? You can't blackmail me about this because Mel's birth and parenthood are fully documented and legal. So bug off."

Roger's face turned a mottled red. "Don't speak to me that way."

"I'll speak to you any way I choose. And don't think you'll get the chance to hit me again either, because you won't."

Roger shoved his face in front of hers. "Do you think big man Stoner is going to get another lucky punch at me? Forget it. I'll have the police on him if he tries."

Tru felt her mouth drop open. "Thane hit you?"

"As if you didn't know."

Tru put her hand to her mouth to smother a bubble of laughter. "I didn't, but I would have given a great deal to see it. By the way, he will be here in less than an hour so maybe you'd better scoot just in case."

"I'm not afraid of him." Roger looked over his shoulder.

"I can see that," Tru ventured dryly. "Get out of here, Roger. You can try anything you want. It won't work. Mel is my child by legal adoption, which has nothing to do with you. If you come near me again, I'll have you charged with harrassment. Get out."

"You haven't heard the last of this, Tru."

"Go."

Tru followed him to the door so that she could slam it behind him and pull the bolt. Then she leaned her back against the door, one hand going to her upper lip to dab at the moisture that had collected there. What could Roger do to her? She and Mel would be in New York.

Thane arrived at eleven forty-five noticing that Tru looked tired and strained, and that the luggage was all neatly stacked at the door.

Without saying a word he went to her and pulled her into his arms. "We argue too much," he said against her hair. "That's one of the things I'd like to change."

"Me too."

"Good. We'll work on it. Get the baby. I'll put the things in the car. I've already had my stuff sent to New York, so we won't have to concern ourselves with that."

"Unless it gets lost."

Thane shrugged. "There are stores in New York."

Mel wasn't as relaxed as she had been the day before and it took everything Tru had to keep her distracted.

The airport was a beehive of activity. People rushed in every direction, narrowly missing each other. Even with Thane handling everything it was fatiguing.

Once on the plane Tru breathed a sigh of relief.

"Shall we put her on the window seat so we can talk more easily?"

Tru nodded, laughing.

"What's so funny?'

"You. You're the only man in the world who can get a skycap by simply cocking an eyebrow. It was very impressive."

"Darling, I'd much rather impress you in other ways." Thane was fully aware that the flight attendant was watching when he kissed Tru on the mouth, but it gave him a sexy kind of satisfaction to disconcert Tru like this.

Tru lay back against the seat, out of breath when he released her.

When the plane taxied down the runway, Tru gazed out the window at the California landscape flying by the window. She and Mel were going back to New York. Would they come to California again? Thane was with them. Happiness zinged through her. The wheels seemed to sing that out as the plane picked up speed.

Yes, life was going to be better. Thane was here. Roger's face flashed in her mind, but Tru blinked away the image. He couldn't hurt them now.

Eight

Living with Thane in New York was at first hard for Tru—she felt hemmed-in. He was everywhere! Bigger than life! Making the spacious brownstone seem like a one-room efficiency.

Juana had been wary of him for about five minutes. Then he'd won her over; while they sat at the kitchen table, talking and laughing.

Tru was dealing with a problem that DENTURES WHILE U WAIT, INC. was having with a customer. "Ah, here it is Mr. Liguorian. Mr. Emmett called you on the fifteenth, not the thirteenth as he thought. If you would like, I could send you a copy of the message. It's no trouble at all. I'm glad to do it. Thank you, Mr. Liguorian. We appreciate the confidence you have in our service." Tru hung up and put her head down on the work table in front of her. She jumped when she felt strong arms lift her from the chair.

"It's been like a zoo around her ever since we got back from California," Thane said, settling his lithe body in her desk chair with Tru in his lap. "You have quite a business."

"What are you doing home so early, anyway?" Tru smothered a yawn with her hand, feeling her body tingle when he massaged her spine.

"Home. Umm, I like that, darling. You're finally coming around to my point of view."

"You don't need my point of view around here. You have Mel and Juana wrapped around your little finger. Isn't that enough?" she asked tartly to compensate for the slip she'd made. Although she hated admitting it, she really *had* begun to think of Thane as living with her.

"The phone never stops ringing when I'm here. I can imagine what it's like when I'm at the office." Thane took her little finger into his mouth and sucked on it sensuously for a moment, his eyes never leaving her face. "Are you having trouble keeping up with it? Maybe I could help."

Tru relaxed against him because she knew that any attempt on her part to free herself would be futile. Thane was so damned good-looking! But though he was cocksure about his ability to handle any situation, business or personal, she knew he wasn't conceited. "Thank you for the offer. I might take you up on it one of these days. It's just a busy time of year, I guess."

Thane nodded. "How would you like a part-time helper in the evenings?"

Tru laughed, trying to get out of his lap, more than aware of the hardening muscles under her. "You! With a multimillion-dollar-corporation to run?"

"Multibillion actually," Thane told her bluntly, amused as he watched her try to free herself. "And yes, darling, you have aroused me, but I'm not letting you off my lap until you promise to go upstairs and shower with me."

"I can't," Tru gasped. "Juana could come upstairs and—"

"I'll tell her not to."

"You'll tell her nothing!" Tru answered back, aghast at what her friend and housekeeper would think if she saw Tru going upstairs to Thane's rooms on the fourth floor. With his usual ease he had called a contractor and a decorator, and in a few days time he'd turned the huge attic into a combination bedroom, sitting room, bath and kitchenette. Tru had been amazed at the results.

Thane kissed her gently on the lips. "Well then, if you won't join me upstairs, I'll just come down to your apartment after Juana goes to bed and we'll shower then."

"You do that anyway," Tru muttered, feeling dizzy as she looked into those bourbon-colored eyes that now had the look of hot bronze.

"Yes, and I'm pretty sure that Juana knows." He shrugged. "Why not give yourself a break and marry me? That way it won't matter what Juana thinks, right?"

"Ah, maybe."

Thane frowned for a moment, then his features relaxed. "You didn't answer me about my offer to help with the business."

"Thank you, but I just hired two women today to handle that. Juana found that things were pretty busy when I was in California, so I put an ad in the paper yesterday and hired two assistants today."

"Good." Thane stood up easily, letting her body slide down his. "I'll go and shower . . . alone. I told Juana I'd help her with the stir fry tonight, so I'd better move. Mel is going to be my assistant." Thane kissed her full on the lips, his mouth moving gently over hers.

Tru had to keep herself from calling him back as he loped across the room and out the door.

Thane had become too important to her. Each

night he came downstairs to her room when the house was quiet and made long, sweet love to her. It both appalled and overjoyed Tru, the way he could wrest passion from the very core of her. There was never any thought of denying him, though. It would have been too much like denying herself.

At dinner Thane diverted them by relating some of the events of his day, and every so often chucked Mel under the chin, making her laugh. When he held the little girl in his arms while they ate, Tru was able to see the amazing likeness between the child's eyes and his. That there was also an affinity between them couldn't be denied.

"She is one happy *muchacha*, Señora Tru," Juana whispered as she put the dessert on the table.

"Yes," Tru agreed, but stopped short of admitting that it was because of Thane.

As usual, that evening after eating they adjourned to the big office in back of the kitchen. Mel was in her playpen, kicking her little legs and working off excess energy before bedtime. Thane was nearby at a desk working from his briefcase, but managing to play with the baby too. Juana sat with her knitting while Tru tended the answering desk, watching, unable to keep from laughing at the way Thane contorted his features for Mel's amusement.

Soon it was time for Mel to go to bed, and as he had done since he'd come from California, Thane accompanied the two women when they bedded down the baby.

"She's so beautiful," Thane whispered when he bent over the crib, the baby holding his large thumb in her tiny fist as she nodded off to sleep.

"Yes," Tru murmured softly at his side, "she is."

"As I told you, Señora Tru," Juana said the next

morning, shortly after eight. Thane had left for work, and the board in the workroom was already lighting up with calls. "I am to go and see my cousin today." Juana pulled on her coat and fur-lined gloves. "Oh, there's my taxi. You will be all right?"

"Just fine." Tru turned the older woman around, urging her toward the front hall. "One of the new assistants is coming in today at four. Now go, and enjoy your visit with your cousin."

"I hate to leave you alone with the baby and the answering service."

Tru knew that a large measure of Juana's reluctance to go was because she hated to leave the baby.

Around mid-morning there was a lull in the calls, and Tru had quite a bit of time to play with Mel and fold the baby clothes that had just come out of the dryer. Since the laundry room was next to the office it was very easy to get everything done.

She was just taking a message from DENTURES WHILE U WAIT when the doorbell rang.

Switching on the message receiver, Tru checked that the baby was secure, then went out to the foyer. She scrutinized the person standing in front of her door through the stained glass side windows, but the man had his back to her, so she couldn't see his face. Opening the door on the chain she shivered as a blast of icy air hit her in the face. "Yes?"

"Hello, Tru. Let me in, will you? It's freezing out here."

"Roger! What do you want?"

"I'm not talking until you open the door and let me in."

Tru was about to tell him to leave, then shrugged and loosened the bolt. Roger was no danger to her now. What was the harm in treating him decently—even if he'd done nothing to deserve it? "I'll give you five minutes to thaw out, then you go. I've very busy."

"The career girl, huh?" Roger shook the snow from his coat, then hung it on the brass coatrack in the foyer.

Tru frowned. "Don't get too comfortable. Just say what you have to and leave."

"Aren't you interested in why I'm in New York?"

"No."

Roger's face turned a dark red. "Well, you will be when I lay it out for you. Heidi and I have a fancy for a place in New York, a cozy little *pied-à-terre* where we can stay if we want to see a show or shop." Roger smiled when he saw her pale. "I see that's got your attention."

"I don't know what you're getting at, Roger, but I do know that I'm too tired to listen while you go on and on. Just get to the point." Tru watched his face mottle angrily. Roger had always been pompous, blindly sure that everyone was interested in what he had to say. The mark of a consummate bore, Tru mused.

Roger looked around the foyer, a tight smile on his lips. "Maybe we could go into the living room and sit down."

"I think not. You won't be staying that long."

"Don't talk to me like that."

"This is my home. I'll talk anyway I choose. Now, will you please say what you have to say and leave."

Roger's face twisted in anger. "My source tells me you're living with Stoner."

Tru went to the door. "I can see I should never have let you in. Now get out."

"I'm not through," Roger snarled. He jabbed his index finger at her. "Since you got this kid when you were still married to me, I intend to sue for my share of her."

Tru staggered back, speechless, stunned by what he said.

Roger looked around him. "This place would suit Heidi and me to a tee . . . and I guess we can negotiate how much of the business proceeds I should get." He looked back at Tru, taking pleasure in her shocked state. "If you don't want to split things with me, I'll take you to court. It shouldn't be too hard to prove you're an unfit mother."

"You're out of your mind," Tru told him hoarsely. "Mel is heir to the business and the house belongs to her. None of this could ever be yours."

"Sorry, Tru honey, but I've talked this over with my lawyer and he seems to think I'd have a good case. Check your divorce papers and you'll find that we weren't legally divorced when you took custody of the child."

"I can see you've done your homework," Tru said, her voice shaking.

"I have." Roger removed a fleck of lint from his sleeve and looked up there, clearly pleased with himself.

"You made a trip to New York just for this. What a fool you are. You won't get away with it and you're out the plane fare." Tru faced him, her hands curled into fists at her sides, struggling to bury the fear that threatened to surface.

"I had to come here for business," Roger told her loftily.

"Then get to it and out of here. You have no chance of getting Mel or the things that belong to her." Tru raised her chin, staring straight at him. Just then Mel let out an angry cry. "Get out of here. I'm busy."

"Pay attention to what I say, Tru," he said, turning back to face her at the huge oak front door, "or you may end up losing that kid. You go out to California, then come back with a live-in lover. Heidi and I are married. We'll be able to care for a child. Come on, Tru, isn't it obvious that if I decide to sue, it won't be difficult to show that you're an unfit mother? You'd lose everything then . . . Hey, maybe you should just sign over the brownstone to me right now. Kind of like settling out of court. I'll even give you a month to get out."

The temerity of the man who'd once been her husband appalled her. She reached for the door-knob so that she could push him out onto the stoop, but then she heard Mel wailing again. Tru's eyes fluttered toward the kitchen, then back to Roger. She couldn't lose Mel even if she lost everything else, and there was no doubt in her mind that Roger would take her to court. "Give me some time to think about it. I have to take care of the baby now."

"Why don't you sign a paper right now? It would save us both a great deal of trouble."

"Go. Or so help me God, I'll call the police and have you arrested for harassment." Tru stared at him through a haze of angry fear.

Roger shot her an ugly look. "I'll call you tomorrow for your decision. If it isn't the right one, I'll get the wheels moving with my lawyer immediately."

"Rat."

Roger moved toward her threateningly, making Tru step back, her eyes scanning the foyer for a weapon. "You'd better be careful what you say to me, or you'll regret it."

With all her might she thrust him out the door and slammed it behind him, then looked down at her trembling hands. She could feel moisture bead-ing on her upper lip. Her mind was a blank. Mel howled again, and Tru rushed to the back of the house, going through the motions of changing the child, dressing and feeding her, like a robot. She put her in the playpen while she went back to work, taking a stream of messages, answering questions, reading off notes to clients.

At the end of three hours of cyclonic activity, with Mel asleep face down in the playpen, Tru went out to the kitchen, put the kettle on for tea and stared at her distorted reflection in the shiny chrome stove. She couldn't remember a single thing she'd done, a person she'd spoken with, or a message she'd taken. "Mel, darling, I can't give you up. I won't even take the chance." Her voice echoed in the stillness.

Juana came home shortly before Thane was due to arrive. "I am sorry, Señora Tru, that I am so late. The buses—" Juana frowned at her. "What is wrong? Are you not feeling well?" Juana fussed over her, holding her palm to Tru's forehead, then grasping Tru's hand. "You will go and rest. The *pequeña* and I will take care of everything."

Tru didn't even argue with her friend. She was too drained.

Once in her bedroom, she stripped off her clothes and slipped under the covers in her bra and panties. Perhaps if she just closed her eyes for a moment she would be able to come up with the solution to her problem.

Thane stared down at Tru as she slept, curled into the fetal position under the sheet.

The moment he'd come in the house Juana had met him with a stream of agitated Spanish, wringing her hands about the señora, who was now lying down.

"Is she ill?" Thane asked.

Juana shrugged. "She has no fever, but something hurts her, in the heart, I think."

Thane had nodded, then strode across the foyer

and up the stairs to the spacious bedroom with the long, narrow Victorian windows at the front of the house. His scrutiny of Tru's room took in everything in seconds: the sheer gold drapes and matching bedspread, the carpet, and finally the figure in the bed.

Thane saw the blue shadows beneath her eyes, not quite masked by the thick fringe of lashes, the way her hands curled under her chin as though she had to protect herself. His insides knotted when he saw how vulnerable she looked. Despite all her bravado, there was a soft center to Tru, a part of herself she rarely let anyone know about, where she hid all hurt.

Someday, he swore to himself now, he'd break down the barriers she'd created around her inner self, and when that day finally came he'd truly have won her.

He studied her sleeping form and shook his head. No one was going to hurt her again. Even if she tried to hide herself from him for the rest of her days, he was going to see to it that she was safe.

Thane dropped his briefcase to the floor and began slowly, methodically, removing his clothes, folding them and putting them on a chair. When he was naked, he climbed into the double bed next to Tru, reaching out to enfold her, bringing her close to him.

She murmured in her sleep, her words slurred and frantic; he crooned love words into her hair, his hands caressing her skin in sweet, concentric circles. "It's all right, darling. I'm here. Relax."

It gave Thane the most profound pleasure when her body straightened out against his, and her hands unclenched, one of them sliding around his waist. "That's right, darling, come close to me." And then she sank into a deep sleep.

Thane was half-asleep when he heard a light knock

at the bedroom door. He barely had time to cover his lower body before Juana cracked it open and put her head through, gazing into Thane's eyes in smiling comprehension. "It is good that she is sleeping, Señor Thane. I have put the baby down for the night. If you need me I will be in my apartment. There is food in the oven."

"Thank you, Juana."

"No, señor, I thank you. Señora Tru has needed you for sometime, I think." She frowned for a moment. "Today, when I returned, she was very bad. Something upset her." The older woman shrugged her shoulders, then backed out of the room and shut the door.

Thane looked down at Tru, his finger tracing the outline of her slightly open lips, feeling the light breath coming between them. Even as he watched her, she inhaled and quivered, her eyes fluttering open, then closed.

Then they snapped open again, fixing on Thane. "Hello. Is it morning?"

Thane kissed her, his mouth moving in passionate search upon hers. "No, it's just past eight, but you've been driving me crazy for over an hour."

Tru wriggled her arm free and squinted at her watch. "Lord, look at the time. Mel has to be put to bed."

"Juana took care of that. She told me that there is food for us when we're ready to eat."

"She told you," Tru echoed faintly, noting the amusement in his eyes.

Thane nodded, kissing her nose. "Juana thinks I'm good for you. So do I. I want us to get married. What do you want?"

Roger's face loomed before Tru's eyes.

"What are you thinking, Tru? You're white as a sheet."

"It's nothing. I'm always a little foggy when I first wake up." Tru blinked at Thane, her mind still on her former husband. She had no doubt that Thane could handle Roger, one-on-one, but Roger wouldn't be that up-front. He'd be underhanded, nasty. And if she told Thane about Roger's latest threats, she knew he'd be so furious that he wouldn't wait to call his lawyer. He'd go out and try to bash Roger's head in. No, for the time being it would be better to say nothing. . . .

"Hey, lady, look at me." Thane's voice was laced with amused irritation. He hated it when Tru was miles away from him, thinking about God knew what. She did that too often. "Juana said that you were very upset when she came home today." Thane's shot in the dark produced an unmistakable quiver in her body. Her eyes slid away from his, her mouth trembled.

Tru pressed her lips tightly together and looked up at him again. "How soon do you think we can get married? I don't want to leave New York to do it and I want Mel with us no matter what."

Thane was shocked by her vehemence; he read desperation in every line of her body. "What's going on, Tru? What aren't you telling me?"

"Do you, or don't you want to marry me?" Her smile was impudent and teasing, but somehow it seemed to him a front.

"I want you any way I can get you," he told her seriously, secretly noting the fact that she wasn't being open with him, that she was hiding from him still. "And it will be a real marriage, Tru! No backing down at the last minute, no more hiding things from me. And don't pretend you haven't been doing just that." He took hold of her and lifted her up, so that she was suspended in his hands. "And I will find out what's eating at you, darling. You can count on that."

"Everyone has secrets," she managed breathlessly.

"Not between us, my sweet. Besides, I'll be keeping you too busy making love. I may even take a year off from work to concentrate on it." Thane watched her closely.

Tru exhaled. "That has to be the sweetest threat in the world."

"When shall we marry? Tomorrow?"

Tru's eyes opened wide and her mouth sagged.

Thane laughed out loud. "We'll make it Friday. That will give you two days to prepare."

"Can we?" Her voice was faint.

"Yes."

She nodded. "Then, Friday it is."

Thane kissed her throat. "Tomorrow Juana can watch Mel and we'll look for rings." He lifted her hand and studied the diamond on her third finger. "This looks beautiful on you."

Tru laughed. "Is your office so organized that you can just drop everything and not show up for days at a time?"

"Very organized."

"Hungry?"

"Yes." Thane laughed out loud when he saw the blood rush into her face. "Disconcerted? About my being hungry for you?"

"Don't make fun of me." Tru shoved at him, then when he was off balance she rolled out of bed and sped across the floor to the bathroom, slamming and locking the door behind her.

Thane was right at her heels banging on the wooden panels. "Hey, no fair. Let me in. I want to take a shower with you."

"Take your own shower," Tru shouted back, then laughed. She didn't notice the scratching and scraping at the bathroom door a few minutes later. She was beginning to shave her legs when she saw the door move. She locked it!

When the heavy oaken door came off its hinges and Thane's face came around the opening, the razor dropped from her hands. "What in hell are you doing?"

"Hi. I think privacy is important to everyone, but I hate it when you shut me out. I just wanted to tell you that." Thane jockeyed the door against the jamb and leaned down to retrieve her razor, smiling at her beguilingly, like a mischievous boy. "I'd love to shave your legs. Will you let me?

"You . . . removed . . . a solid oak door to tell me . . . that . . ." Tru sputtered, words failing her as she looked up at him. Behind his smile she saw his steely determination. "How will you ever get it up again?"

"Easy. Now, seeing how much trouble I went to to get in here, may I join you?"

Tru felt herself melting. If he continued to look at her that way, she would end up by throwing herself on his chest and blurting out everything. "Maybe. First put up the door and I'll shower." The blatant disappointment in his face sent a wave of remorse through her. "Ah, but you might release the lock so that you can come in and join me in the shower." Tru was suddenly throbbing with excitement at the bright sensuousness of his smile.

Trembling, she stepped into the huge claw-footed tub and drew the shower curtain all around.

"Here I am." Thane grinned at her.

Tru looked around him. "How did you get that door up so fast? It won't fall, will it?"

Thane gave her a dark look. "I worked on a construction crew for two summers during school. I helped hang steel doors larger than that."

"Sorry, I didn't know I was talking to King Kong."

"Lady, you're baiting me." Thane yanked at the shower curtain, cocooning them. "Punishment time." He scooped her up in one arm clamping her tight to his body, letting her stomach come to rest against his aroused lower body.

"This is punishment?" she joked, her heart careening against her chest at the flare of heat in his eyes.

"You like it, my sweet?"

"Only at your hands."

Thane eased her down his body until they were joined intimately. Her eyes widened in sexy awareness, their sapphire hue deepening, before they closed in slow, sweet acceptance of him. Thane massaged her flesh gently. "Making love with you like this is incredibly erotic."

Tru nodded, her eyes still closed, her throat too dry for words.

In strong, slow, sure thrusts the rhythm of love took them again. They gasped in ragged concert. Nothing existed on the planet but the two of them.

Tru cried out against Thane's neck as they climaxed together. "Never . . . never did I know about such feelings, Thane." Tru's face slid against the hot moistness of his skin.

"It's new for me too, angel."

"No."

"Yes."

Finally they washed each other, gazes locked. They kissed often, hands never ceasing caressing. When at last Thane helped her out of the tub, his touch was protective, possessive. Even toweling dry became a sweet encounter. Words were unnecessary.

"I love you," Thane told her casually.

"What?"

"You heard me, very plainly."

"Oh." Tru tingled with joy from toe to eyebrow; she felt lighter than she ever had before.

Thane watched as she walked ahead of him into the bedroom, her supple, slender, tall body gliding forward in swaying grace. Gazing at her walk he experienced all the power that beautiful women wield. He recalled the first time he'd entered the Louvre and stood in front of the Mona Lisa, how his breath had left him. A similar awe held him now as his eyes ran up the long legs to the swell of hip, the soft indentation of her waist, the alluring curve of her breast barely showing.

When Tru whirled around looking for her fleecy robe, she caught his gaze, then laughed out loud. 'You'll never eat if you keep this up."

Thane closed his eyes, shaking his head. "I know. I don't believe this. I could make love to you again. Not even at twenty did I have this sexual drive."

"Poor baby."

"Get dressed, siren."

Tru smiled up at him, feeling no discomfort at shedding her robe, getting underthings from a dresser and donning them.

"I'll be right back." Pulling on the trousers of his suit he took his things and left the room in long strides.

Tru didn't take her eyes off the door as she dressed in a teal blue velour jumpsuit with cuffed sleeves and a mandarin collar.

When she heard his footsteps, she took a deep breath. "There. I'm dressed and I couldn't be more covered." Tru laughed.

Thane was still pulling a ribbed cotton sweater over his head. "You'd look sexy in nun's habit, so don't think you've cooled me down. Come on, woman, let's eat. I'm starved."

In the kitchen they heated the bouillabaisse Juana

had made, and took a spinach salad, ready and waiting for them, from the fridge.

"Umm, bouillabaisse from a Spanish cook. What could be better?" Thane spooned some of the hot fish stew into his mouth.

"It's one of my favorites and it was one of Maggie's too. . . ."

They ate in silence then, and as they did Tru remembered Roger and the awful threats he'd made earlier in the day. What if Roger really was able to prove the nasty allegations he'd made against her? Tru had to protect Mel at all costs. She only had to imagine Mel with Roger to break out in a cold sweat.

"You're hiding from me again, Tru."

"I know, and there is so much that you have a right to know, but I would rather wait until after we're married before we discuss any of it."

"Most good relationships are built on openness, aren't they?" Thane asked her evenly.

"That's true."

"I trust you. Do you trust me?"

"Yes."

Thane noted how she pressed her lips tightly together as though the affirmation pained her. "Why do I get the feeling that your trust is paper-thin?"

Tru lifted her chin. "I don't know."

Thane saw the misery etched in her face. "I won't press you, Tru. We'll be marrying in a few days. I can wait until then."

"Thank you." She felt her chin wobble, as she blinked back the salty sting of tears.

In silence they cleaned up, stacking the rinsed dishes in the dishwasher, scouring the one pan they'd used, and tidying up the kitchen so that Juana would not have that chore in the morning.

Tru hung up the towel they'd been using, looked once around the kitchen, avoiding Thane's eyes, then preceded him out of the room, hearing him click off the light.

Thane followed behind her, getting the same sense of pleasure watching her move when she was dressed as he had when she'd walked in front of him nude.

Tru turned at the door of the bedroom, her mouth opening to speak.

"Forget it sweetheart, I'm coming in with you."

"I thought you'd be tired."

"We're sleeping together," he said, his tone brooking no opposition. "I'll check Mel, shall I?"

"I'll go with you."

"Fine."

They walked along the short corridor to the baby's room, their bodies bumping gently, their hands touching but not clinging.

Tru bent over the crib, checking the baby for dampness, then changing her quickly, so that the child's sleep was barely disturbed.

Thane watched the metamorphosis in Tru's face, which suddenly shone with a look that was beatifically maternal. It took his breath away. "Madonna," he murmured.

Tru tucked the baby's blanket around her sleeping form, then turned her head toward Thane. "What did you say?" she whispered.

"Talking to myself." Thane leaned down and lightly patted Mel's bottom. When they were strolling back to the master bedroom, Thane slipped his arm around her waist. "I like children. I think we should have more than one. What do you think?"

Tru felt her body suffuse with heat. "I think a family would be wonderful."

"Should we start ours at once?"

"At once?"

Thane studied her upturned face as he ushered

her into the bedroom. "Is there some reason we shouldn't have children right away?"

"Well, there is the business . . ." Tru floundered.

"You have assistants to help you with that."

"True."

"Anything else?"

"Maybe we should get to know each other better before we have children."

"And I think kids should be close in age so that they have more in common."

"There is that." Tru eyed him warily.

"Good. We agree. We'll start our family . . . tonight."

Before she could stop him, or even get out a word, Thane unzipped her jumpsuit and peeled it off, kissing her and pushing her back on the bed.

"I really do love doing this." Then Thane's mouth covered hers in a deep soul stealing kiss.

At that moment, Tru not only forgot her impulse to hold him back, she couldn't recall why she ever would have wanted to.

Nine

Tru awoke on her wedding day woolly-headed and still not sure how everything had been arranged. Amazed, she stared across the room at the clothes tree with the long cream-colored silk dress she and Thane had picked out at Bergdorf Goodman. Tiny silk orange blossoms no bigger than her baby fingernail dotted the tight bodice and the hem of the full skirt.

She sighed as she got out of bed. Soon the florist would arrive with the real orange blossoms that Juana would weave into the wreath for her hair.

"It's a fantasy," Tru whispered to herself, ". . . happening too fast." A tear made its way down her cheek. "Ellen isn't even going to be my attendant. It's insane." She wiped her cheek, then got ready to shower and change. Soon she'd wrapped herself in a steamy cocoon, blotting from her mind everything but the tactile enjoyment of the warm water sluicing down her body.

Thane got off the phone, grimacing at the dark

silk suit he'd chosen to wear. When he reached for his tie, his hand shook. He stared down at it. Wanting and needing Tru had consumed him for the past five days. Now, in less than two hours he'd actually be marrying her. Though Thane wasn't fool enough to think that marriage would solve all their problems, he knew it had to come first. Once she was Gertrude Stoner, he could protect her. Then little by little Tru would begin to feel safe.

The phone rang at his elbow, jerking him to attention. He sucked air into his lungs unsteadily. "Yes?"

"It's Ellen. We're all on our way to the church. I'm so excited I could die."

"Don't do that. Tru has been going around the house with her lip quivering all week, telling me that it would be foolish to ask you to come East on such short notice."

There was noise at the end of the line as Ellen repeated what Thane said, then a rush of unintelligible comments.

"Hey, buddy, I heard that. Doesn't your bride-to-be know that you could buy Nevada and make change?" Andy chuckled.

"Funny. Just be at the church to stand at my side."

"I wouldn't miss this if I were in a body cast. I can hear the sobs of the broken-hearted ladies coming all the way from the West Coast."

"See you soon." Thane hung up the phone, smiling grimly at the receiver. It had been a stroke of luck that he had been able to fly all of Ellen's family to New York. His own family was here too, staying at the same hotel. They had arrived last night. More than once he'd almost told Tru about all the old friends and relatives who would be coming, but he'd managed to resist the urge. He wanted it to be a surprise wedding present from him.

The weather cooperated, with a blinding sun, blue sky, and crystals of snow falling on the pavement. It was cold, but beautifully clear, and the city glistened as though it had been painted in gold.

Later, after they'd both dressed, Thane was watching Tru from the hallway as she went to the foyer and studied the prisms of sunlight streaming in the stained glass of the old-fashioned front door. She could hear Juana in the kitchen talking to Mel as she fed the baby a snack before leaving for the church.

Church! It had surprised Tru when Thane told her that they would be married by a clergyman, and not in a judge's chambers as she had assumed.

"You look gorgeous, like a Viking princess, and I want you very much."

The whispered words behind her went through her clothes and entered her bloodstream. Even with her back to him she could see Thane. He made her weak, yet the urges he ignited within her had enough force to burn down a building. All her longings and hungers had gathered into one surge toward this man, and she couldn't stem the flood.

Whirling, her skirt swinging out around her ankles, she faced him. "I have the feeling I look more like a gypsy than a bride."

Thane held out his arms. "Dance, gypsy."

Tru floated toward him, her own arms uplifted, much of the depression she'd felt threatening to rise, dissipating at the sight of him. "Have we time?"

"There is always time for a gypsy to dance. It's her destiny."

"You believe so strongly in fate?"

"Since I met you, yes." Thane began to hum the strains of the *Zigeuner.*

"You even come equipped with music for the occasion?"

"How can you ask such a question? You think

you're dealing with some rank amateur? Every bride needs music when she's dancing on her wedding morning."

"I didn't even know that brides danced on their wedding morning."

"You've led a sheltered life, I can see that. Marriage will be very broadening for you."

Helpless laughter flowed from Tru as Thane whirled her around the foyer, their feet clicking rhythmically on the parquet floor.

"What is this?" Juana came through from the kitchen holding Mel, who chuckled when Thane passed her and made kissing noises at her. "Shame on you, Señor Thane. It is not right for you to see the bride before the ceremony." Juana tried to look severe, but she was laughing as convulsively as Tru.

"Stop. Stop. I'm out of breath." Tru clung to his neck, her feet leaving the floor as he lifted her close.

"That's it, sweetheart, now you're learning. Hang onto me. That's what I want you to do always." Thane kissed her quickly, then lowered her gently. "Let's go, ladies. We have to get to the church." He gave Juana a mock frown. "It isn't easy getting three beautiful women moving." Then he kissed the baby. "And my Mel looks so wonderful in her blue velvet dress."

"Oh Señor Thane, you are one *macho hombre*," Juana simpered, bustling Mel into her winter coat and hat.

"Where are you going, Tru? I have your coat." Thane whisked a full-length sable from a box on a chair in the foyer.

Tru stared at the shimmering folds of the coat. "I've never seen anything so lovely! It's exquisite, Thane."

"Wear it today, darling, please."

Tru turned around so that he could lay the full

length sable across her shoulders. She inhaled deeply. "It feels . . . sinful."

Thane chuckled and kissed her neck before turning to Juana. "Let me take the baby. The driver should be out front by now."

Tru gasped at the chauffeur-driven Rolls Royce in front of the brownstone. "My goodness. We are going in style."

"Do I have to keep reminding you that this is your wedding day?"

"No." Tru thought of Ellen for a moment and the lengthy letter she'd written her friend in California about getting married, and how she'd miss not having her at the wedding. Then she pushed it from her mind and smiled at Thane.

Juana looked around her, from her place on the middle seat, smiling. "This is a macho car, too, I think, Señor Thane."

Thane laughed out loud, kissing the baby's forehead. He and Tru sat together in the back seat.

They were to be married in the Little Church Around the Corner in the heart of Manhattan. It wasn't far, but after a few minutes Tru began to feel as though she had been confined in the limousine for days. Her breathing became shallow and she couldn't stop threading her fingers together.

Thane noticed her growing agitation and placed his free hand over hers. "Juana, will you hold Mel for a moment?"

"Of course, Señor Thane." Juana cradled the child Thane handed to her.

Thane reached for Tru and wrapped her in his arms. "Everything is fine. No need for you to fret."

"I know." She gave him a weak smile. "I'm acting silly." She stared up at him. "I am glad I'm marrying you, and I don't have any reason to be nervous."

"But you are."

"Yes."

Thane kissed her hair. "So am I."

Startled, Tru gazed into his eyes, seeing the slumberous heat there. "Really?"

"Yes. Even though you're the only woman I've ever wanted to marry. I want it to last, to grow, to change, yet always be the same. It's a daunting prospect."

"Very. You know, it's funny, but if I think about it, I realize I have no reason to trust marriage."

"That's because you've never had a good one."

Tru put her head on his shoulder, nodding. The car pulled over to the curb and stopped. Tru leaned forward in the seat and looked through the grillwork to the church, snow patterning the slate roof and the old stone facade.

Thane got out of the car, helping the ladies to alight. As they entered the vestibule at the back of the church, Tru blinked against the dimness after the bright sunlight.

"Surprise, old friend," Ellen whispered, coming up to Tru and hugging her. "Did you really think I would let you go through this without me?"

"Ellen . . . Randy . . . Andrew." Tru reeled in delighted shock as all the Sandilins came forward to hug her. "I didn't know." She turned to Thane. "What a wonderful . . ." She pressed her hand to her mouth, not wanting to cry on her wedding day. "Thane, thank you. I love you." She felt him stiffen under her hands when she put them on his shoulders and leaned up to kiss him.

"Darling," he breathed, half irked when his sister tugged at his sleeve and demanded to be introduced. "Go away, Linda."

"Barbarian. Introduce me to your bride. Mother and Dad are convinced she is the only woman on earth who could tame you. She must be an Amazon."

"Linda, why doesn't Damon strangle you?" Thane

asked his sister lazily, ready to do the job himself because she'd intruded on a very important moment between Tru and himself.

"I do get a wrestling hold on her whenever I can," Damon Struthers told his brother-in-law. "But maybe that's not what you mean, is it, Whizzer? How are you, Tru? It's a real pleasure to meet you."

"Thank you. It's nice to meet all of you." She turned to Thane. "Whizzer? Was that your nickname when you played football?"

Thane nodded, smiling crookedly.

"I, for one, am insulted that nobody let me hold a dinner party for the bride-to-be." Linda Struthers gave Thane a sharp look.

"Now, Linda, do be sensible." Mrs. Stoner kissed Tru's cheek.

"Not in a million years would I let you do that to Tru, subject her to the stampede of cattle you call friends, at the club," Thane remarked.

"Ape," Linda pronounced mildly. "Ah, there's the baby. She is lovely."

"Isn't she? Getting ideas, Linnie?" Damon whispered.

"Maybe." Linda studied Tru. "Your coat is sensational, Tru."

Thane hugged Tru and removed the sable.

"Separate, you two. Here comes the minister," Mrs. Sandilin informed them, laughing. "Come Juana, let's take the baby to the pew."

"Sí, I will go with you," Juana told the other woman, her dark eyes snapping with excitement.

"Come along, groom. If I recall the drill, we go this way." Andrew yanked Thane away from Tru and led him toward the altar.

"My dear, I hope you won't mind if I give you away. I did so want the job."

"Oh, Mr. Sandilin, I'd love for you to."

Ellen fussed with Tru's dress, looking at her, distressed. "I wasn't this jumpy even at my own wedding. Randy, keep an eye on me. If I lose it, pinch me."

"You'll knock 'em dead, my love." Randy kissed his wife and Tru, then went to take his seat with the others.

When the organist struck the opening chords of *Lohengrin*, Tru and Mr. Sandilin followed Ellen down the short aisle to the front.

The sacred words the minister spoke resounded in the church. When Thane put the ring on her finger, Tru couldn't take her eyes from it for a moment, and the minister had to clear his throat to get her to perform the same office for Thane.

"We're married, darling," Thane whispered as he bent to kiss her. "You belong to me now and I'll never let you go."

"Please don't." Tru gave him a waivering smile, then turned at his urging to see the faces of her friends as they returned to the vestibule.

Thane hustled them all into the limousines standing at the curb, and in moments they were weaving through midtown traffic, their destination a private club called The Windsor which Thane had booked for the wedding luncheon.

"And where will you be going on your honeymoon?" the irrepressible Ellen asked as soon as everyone was seated at a large round table in the club.

"We're not taking a trip yet," Thane answered.

"Please take her to Hawaii, Thane. Go to our beach house on Maui. You can leave Mel with us," Mrs. Sandilin urged.

"You must, Thane. Mother has talked non-stop about Mel since my wedding." Ellen rolled her eyes.

"Mel is to blame for many things." Andrew grinned at Clare, who blushed prettily. "My wife intended to be a career woman before she spotted her. Now we will have our own baby in seven months or so."

Tru sat back and watched as they all congratulated Clare and Andrew, everyone talking at once and laughing. Tru felt comforted, warm, as if in the midst of her very own family. The Sandilins had always been like a real family to her . . . and then there were the Stoners. The many fears she'd had about them faded as she watched them together, bantering amiably. She cared for Thane's mother and father very much and had the feeling she would get on well with his sister and brother-in-law.

Then, though, the specter of Roger rose in front of her. If only she didn't have him to think about, the day would have been perfect.

"Shall we dance, Mrs. Stoner?"

"That's me," Tru said softly.

"Indeed it is . . . forever."

The small trio that Thane had engaged for the afternoon played "The Hawaiian Wedding Song."

"I think Maui sounds like a good idea . . . maybe in a month. What do you think?"

"Do you think we could get away?" Tru asked breathlessly.

"Of course. My staff is efficient and Juana handles your business beautifully now."

"Right." Tru could feel herself weakening.

"Well?"

"I think it sounds wonderful."

"Darling."

Tru leaned her head against his strong chest and closed her eyes. She could have glided around the floor with Thane forever.

"Happy, darling?"

Tru nodded. "Very. I always forget how much Ellen's family means to me until I'm with them." She looked up at him. "That was so kind of you."

Thane felt dizzy with happiness because Tru's eyes were on him, wide open, warm, giving, the way he'd wanted them to be. If there was a shadow there, he could banish it, as long as they were together.

"May I cut in?" Thane's father smiled at his son.

"We just started," Thane complained.

"Thane." Tru shook her head, half laughing.

Cranston Stoner eased Tru away from him and glided with her across the room. "I suppose he wants to punch me in the nose," he told Tru amusedly. "That's what I would have wanted to do if anyone had cut in on me and my Liddie."

"Ah, so you're teasing him." Tru grinned at her father-in-law.

"Yes, and enjoying every minute of it. Thane has had an independent streak a mile wide ever since he was about three years old . . . always moving forward, over every obstacle . . . until he met you." He kissed Tru's forehead. "Thane was a stranger to humility until then, I fear. My goodness, what a setback you were for him . . ." He paused for a moment to reflect before going on. "You have been very good for him, even when you went East shortly after the two of you met. We were so sure he was going to stay in New York with you, that we would have bet our house on it." A crease appeared between Cranston Stoner's eyes. "He never did tell us why he returned in such a hurry . . . or became such a bear afterwards. He was pretty impossible for quite a while." Cranston smiled all at once. "Ah, here's Andrew coming to claim you."

"Mr. Stoner . . ."

"Call me Cranston, dear."

"All right, thank you." Tru shot a quick glance at Andrew and hurried her words. "Ah, I never knew Thane came to New York. . . . Maybe it was for business. You see, the first time we had any contact at all in almost a year was when I went West to be in Ellen's wedding."

"Really?" Mr. Stoner's brows knit. "Well, if you had no contact with him, what could have set off that binge of hard living he went on? . . ."

Andrew tapped Mr. Stoner on the shoulder. "Shame on you, sir, monopolizing the bride."

"You're right, Andrew. Your turn."

"Wait," Tru called to the older man as Andrew whisked her back onto the dance floor.

"My feelings are hurt. You prefer Thane's father to me."

"Damn you, Andrew, he was telling me something about Thane . . . that he came to New York shortly after I arrived."

Andrew shuddered noticeably. "You don't want to know anything about Thane then. He was a madman. He partied all night, then went home, changed his clothes and went to his office, sometimes working twelve hours a day. He shunned his old friends. It wasn't pretty."

Tru felt all the blood leave her face. "You're making this up."

Andrew shook his head, his smile rueful. "He's been my best friend for years, but during those wild months I gave him a wide berth. He even drank too much, and believe me, he can hold his booze, and dated scads of different women."

"Really." Tru felt a stab of jealousy.

"Ouch. Tru, you're digging your damn nails into my arm." Andrew chuckled. "You two really get to each other. You're like two sticks of dynamite."

"Yes," Tru muttered. The thought of Thane surrounded by a coterie of women stuck like a bitter stone in her chest. Even though she'd walked away from him, it made her furious to think how easy it had been for him to find consolation. "I could kill him," she muttered, the vicious intensity of her words stunning her, her eyes flying to Andrew's amused face.

"Wow. Deliver me from such hot-blooded people."

"May I have my wife back?" Thane's handsome face appeared suddenly behind Andrew's shoulder.

"Of course. Give me a head start, though, will you, because I know you'll be coming after me once you find out that I told Tru all about your deep, dark past." Andrew laughed at Thane's scowl, then meandered back to the table.

"What's he talking about?"

"Did you come to New York looking for me after I left California to come and stay with Maggie and Tom?" Tru went straight for the jugular.

Thane's hold on her tightened. "How did that come up?"

"Did you?"

"Yes."

Tru felt her mouth open in shock. "You never told me."

"You never asked."

"Why did you come?"

"I should think that would be obvious."

Tru had stopped dead in her tracks. "You spied on me in New York."

"I saw you once," Thane answered savagely. "Now I think we'd better drop this. My sister is headed our way and you look as though I just pushed you under a bus."

Tru stared up at him blindly, her knees feeling weak.

"Whatever did you say to her, Thane?" Linda drawled. "She's downright chalky."

Thane bared his teeth at his sister but stayed silent.

"Wedding nerves," Tru offered limply.

"Dear me." Linda looked intently from her brother to Tru. "Why don't we go to the ladies' room and fix our faces, Tru?"

"Fine."

"I'm warning you, Lin, don't badger her." Thane's voice was hoarse.

"Thane, you've become boorish in your old age," his sister said sharply, leading Tru away.

In the powder room Tru bathed her hot face with cool water, but somehow she couldn't seem to rid herself of the feverish feeling. Today had been happy up until now. But suddenly she felt woefully confused. Thane had come to New York. But he'd never contacted her. What could his motives have been? Her growing feeling of security with Thane began to fade. She felt bereft and vulnerable.

"What's wrong?" Linda fired at her as soon as the door swung closed.

"Nothing. It's been a long day, that's all."

"Look, Tru, I know you love my brother. I could see it when you recited your vows. So what's wrong?"

Tru gazed at the other woman in the mirror, and shook her head.

"Something's happened. What is it? You can tell me." Linda put her hands on Tru's arms and turned her so that they were face to face.

"Yes, but . . . this is something I have to work through by myself." Tru made herself smile and then kissed Linda on the cheek. "Just believe that what you saw at the church is true. I do love your brother."

"Good. Mother and Daddy say he's bonkers about you."

An unsteady laugh broke from Tru and she held out her hand to the other woman. "Thanks for helping me pull myself together. I needed your support."

"Getting away from men is sometimes the only way to do it."

Tru laughed more naturally just as the door opened.

"Oh there you are, girls. It's time to go." Mrs. Stoner beamed at them.

Tru followed Linda and her mother out to the main room, still feeling shaky, but smiling bravely nonetheless.

"Tomorrow we'll have lunch with everyone before they return to the coast," Thane said as he appeared at her side.

"Good."

"And I will go to my cousin's this evening, Señora Tru. Mrs. Sandilin and Mrs. Stoner wish to take the baby to the hotel with them. Is fine, no?"

"Take Mel away?" Tru felt her jaw drop and her stomach lurch.

"You don't have to give Mel to them if you don't want to," Thane said in a flat voice. "I think, though, that they just want us to have some time alone."

"Oh, don't say no, Tru." Linda laughed, staring right into Tru's eyes as though she were signaling to her.

"Please, Tru. We want to spoil her again." Mrs. Sandilin sent Mrs. Stoner a conspiratorial smile.

"All right, but you must . . ."

"Not to worry, Señora Tru, I will tell them all they need to know."

Thane put an arm around Juana. "Both of us would be happier if you would go to the hotel with the family, Juana. There's a room for you just down the hall from my parents."

"Señor, I could not . . ." Juana's hands flew into the air in flustered surprise.

"We would love to have you, Juana. Then you could tell us all the stories about Mel that we don't know," Mrs. Stoner cajoled.

Juana's gaze flew to Tru, who nodded. "Go on,

Juana. Call your cousin and tell her you'll come another time."

Juana nodded, her eyes bright.

The party broke up slowly with the guests drifting toward the exits and the limousines that would take them back to the hotel.

Tru sat next to Thane on the way home looking out her window, aware that he was looking out his, avoiding her studiedly. They didn't speak at all, but when they reached their front door, Thane gave the driver a large tip and helped Tru out of the car.

Tru stood back to let him unlock the heavy front door with its stained glass panels. When he swept her up into his arms after pocketing her key, she gasped in alarm.

"Did you forget that the bride is supposed to be carried over the threshold?"

"I suppose I did."

"I didn't." Once in the foyer, he allowed her to slide down his body. He kissed her once very lightly on the mouth and released her. "Are you hungry?"

"After all those canapés and that big dinner? No. I don't think I'll eat for a week."

A half smile played at Thane's lips. "Then why don't we change and I'll start a fire in the fireplace and we can listen to some music. If we get hungry later, we can raid the refrigerator. How does that sound?"

"Good. I'll join you after I change." Tru went up the stairs to her room and directly to the adjoining bath, where she started the water running in the tub before removing her clothes. As the room filled with steam, she unthreaded the orange blossoms from her hair, then drew her silky white slip down over her breasts and hips, leaving her standing before the mirror in her panties and gartered stockings.

"You're quite lovely, wife."

Tru spun around to see Thane in the doorway with his arms full of clothing. She stared at the mound of shirts and suits he dropped on the bed, forgetting her nakedness.

"You *did* assume that we would share a bedroom, didn't you?"

"Of course, but . . ."

"I just brought down a few things for now."

"Whatever," Tru said tartly.

Thane stared at the slender form, wanting her very much. "You'll catch cold, Tru," he said simply.

"I was just going to take a bath."

"I'll join you." He watched her turn and clutch the doorknob. "You don't want me to take the door off again, do you?"

"No."

"Good."

Tru felt like running from him—but there was nowhere to run. She'd felt this way ever since talking to Andrew and Cranston. She climbed into the tub, sinking down into the steamy depths, the unaccustomed luxury of not having to hurry making her eyelids droop.

The bathroom door banged open; she felt a draft, then heard his voice.

"All right, sweet wife, now tell me why you froze up at our wedding reception."

Ten

Tru hunched down deep in the water, feeling determination crackle in the thick air of the bathroom. "I don't know what you mean."

"You're hedging," he shot back. "After you danced with my father and Andrew you went around with a dazed look in your eyes. You face was paper white. Was it just because you discovered that I had come to New York?"

"If we have something to discuss, shouldn't we do it in the living room?"

"More hedging," Thane muttered, stepping into the claw-footed tub and lowering his strong muscular body into the fragrant suds. "Did you have to drown us in essence?"

"You didn't have to get in my bath."

"Gertrude!"

Tru jumped, splashing water up over the lip of the tub. "You bellowed, my lord?"

"Tell me what was said to you, all of it."

Tru stared at him for long minutes. "You probably won't answer my questions anyway."

"I already did answer the questions you asked me at the Windsor."

"Why didn't you get in touch with me when you came to New York?"

"I saw you. You didn't see me," Thane said quietly.

"That's damned cryptic," Tru cried.

A pained look came into his eyes. He lowered his head, shaking it slowly back and forth.

"What is it?" Tru whispered.

There was a long silence while Thane fought off an onslaught of unhappy memories. "I came to New York to convince you to come back to California with me," Thane finally said. "I was so damned sure I'd succeed that I never even bothered to call." Sharply sucking in a breath of air, he continued. "I drove here very early one morning. Parking the car down the block I rehearsed what I would say to you. There wasn't a doubt in my mind that you would be with me on the plane back. Then the front door opened and two people came out on the steps. One of them was you and the other was a man I didn't know. Both of you were laughing. Then he kissed you and you put your arms around his neck." He laughed harshly. "I learned about pain then. Everything in me stopped . . . and I had to get away."

Tru shook her head back and forth. "You're crazy."

"Am I?"

"Yes, you saw me kiss Tom, Maggie's husband," Tru explained desperately, watching the emotions her words evoked dig into the flesh of his face, changing it, remolding it.

"I figured that out some months later when I came out of my blue period long enough to study the information that Billy had given me, and put two and two together."

"You sent someone to find me?"

Thane nodded.

"And yet you never came up to the door, rang the bell and asked me about the man who had kissed me on the doorstep?"

"Right again."

Fury mushroomed in her! He had assumed that she had found someone else as soon as she left him. He thought so little of her! "Andy said you were impossible to live with after I left for New York." Tru dropped the words like a gauntlet between them, goading him to react.

His eyes flared at her words. She was sure, for a second, that he was going to strike her, and she balled her fists in defense.

"Do you want a blow-by-blow account of my debacle?" His query was silky, but there was lightning in his eyes.

"Of course," Tru countered daringly, blinking when he caused a wave of water to sweep up the sides of the tub. In one swift move he scooped her up and settled her in his lap. "What are you doing?" she gasped.

"We should be closer. I don't want you to miss a word." Thane licked the outer edge of her ear. "Comfy, wife?"

"Yes." Tru's voice came from someplace deep in her throat.

"You sound unsure."

"Get on with it," she told him through her teeth. Tru could feel his body hardening under hers.

"All right." Thane kissed her throat, his lips lingering there, putting just a bit more pressure on the pulse that fluttered at its base. He pulled back from her a bit, his eyes on her face. "As Andy said, it wasn't a great time in my life. I don't remember much about that return flight from New York, except that I drank a great deal and managed to make dates with both flight attendants." Thane flinched

when she dug her nails into his neck, but his voice
continued on, even and uninflected. "I decided on
the way back to California that you'd just been string-
ing me along. Consequently, by the time I landed
was a powder keg about to blow." Thane's face twisted
as he went on. "My life was crazy from there on.
crammed twice as much work as humanly possible
into each day. My employees began to duck when
they saw me coming. Nights were a blur of partying,
drinking, women." He gave a hard laugh.

"Lots of women."

"Lots of everything." He shifted her in his arms so
that he could look into her face. "Are you sure you
want to hear this?"

"No, but tell me anyway."

"I woke up one morning in Las Vegas and I was
sure I'd married the woman next to me in bed." He
paused when he felt her stiffen. "You wanted to hear
this, wife."

"So I did." Tru flexed her fingers, her mouth as
dry as a desert.

"That was when I decided that I would find out for
myself what was going on with you, face you with it
shake the truth out of you if I had to. I was sick to
death of trying to blot out the image of you with that
other man. So I sobered up, flew back to Los Angeles
alone and began to get my life on track again . .
and plan how I was going to win you back.

"From new reports that Billy sent me I knew that
you were living by yourself. I wasn't keeping in contact with the Sandilins at the time, so I didn't know
about Maggie's death."

Tru was staring at him now. "Go on."

Thane smiled in amused comprehension. "Adding
things up in that convoluted mind of yours? Don't
bother. You usually come to the wrong conclusion."

"Is that so?" Tru twisted around, threading her hands through his hair and yanking.

"Ouch, wife, that hurts, but it also turns me on, so don't stop." Thane undulated his body under hers, laughing when he saw her color rise. "You're annoyed by what I just told you."

"Partly." Tru watched him closely, running more hot water as what was in the tub became tepid. "You claimed that Mel was your baby. Did you ever believe that? Really?"

Thane inhaled deeply. "You are asking some big questions." Thane nodded. "When I saw Mel, it just exploded in my mind that she had my eyes and your hair. I guess I wanted it so much that I figured it had to be true. I did believe it until my better judgment took over."

"And how long did that take?"

"At our second meeting I was pretty sure the baby wasn't yours . . . or mine." Thane watched the subtle changes of expression in her face, the color rise in her cheeks.

"Yet you kept badgering me about the baby being yours."

Thane shrugged. "If you're waiting for an apology, forget it. I would have done a lot more if needed."

"Ruthless."

"Yes." He touched her chin. "Hey, did you just shiver?"

"The water has cooled," she told him softly.

"Almost as much as you have." Thane leaned forward and turned on the hot water again. Then, ignoring her protests, he began washing her.

In minutes Thane had pulled her to her feet next to the tub, swaddling her in a bath sheet and drying her completely. Then he poured oil from a bottle on the vanity into his hands and patted it into her skin

from ankle to neck. "There. Shall I get the negligee
my sister gave you?"

Tru nodded, noting from the stubborn set of his
chin that it would be useless to argue. "How did you
remember about Linda's gift?"

"I've been visualizing you in it since it came."

Thane left the bathroom but was back in minutes,
the filmy garment over his arm, his naked body
seeming impervious to chill. "There, shall I help you
with it?" The wicked look in his eyes cut through
her, as though he could see through the voluminous
towel to the body beneath.

"It's too crowded with both of us trying to dress
in here. Why don't you dry off here and I'll dress in
the bedroom." Tru went past him, the negligee over
her arm.

"Coward."

Tru lifted her chin, her body jerking when she felt
his feather-light touch on her towel-wrapped buttocks. She was still shaken by his disclosures. She
stood in the middle of the bedroom for a moment
unable to function. Finally she sighed, staring at
the door leading to the bathroom, her thoughts a
jumble as she dropped her towel.

Twisting the damp strands of her hair into a knot
on her head and pinning it loosely, she donned the
silk nightgown with the spaghetti straps that matched
the peignoir. A sudden tremor shook her as the
sensuous material slithered down her body. Facing
the mirror she pushed her feet into the high-heeled
silk mules that had come with the negligee.

"You're beautiful, wife."

Tru whirled to face him, feeling the fine fabric
billow out around her, then settle back on her like a
wispy caress.

Thane was propped against the door jamb, his
hair wet and glistening ebony in the light from the

desk lamp nearby, his sherry-colored robe coming just to the knees of his muscular legs. Black hair showed on his chest at the opening of the robe; his body was tanned and tough looking.

To Tru he looked like a sophisticated pirate. In a sudden wish to see the bourbon lightning flash in his eyes again, she twirled slowly. "Like it?"

"Elegant, sexy, gorgeous. . . . What more could a man ask?"

Tru faced him, breathless. It struck her suddenly that she should take this opportunity to tell him about Roger, but somehow she couldn't bring herself to do so on her wedding night. The thought of her ex-husband rose like bile in her throat. She swallowed, and pushed Roger to the back of her mind. "You look like a svelte brigand."

Thane's eyebrow cocked. "And are you my booty?"

His whispered words reached out and coiled around her. "I . . . think maybe I am."

Thane strolled toward her, his hands palm upward, as though he was allowing himself to be vulnerable to her. "Then unless you have an objection, I claim you."

"No objection," Tru whispered huskily.

"Darling! My Wife!" Thane muttered the words like a solemn vow, as though the very sound of them could spur his emotions.

Then Tru felt him lift her up close to his chest, cradling her there, their mouths centimeters apart, hearts pounding breast to breast.

"I hate to remove that negligee. It looks so wonderful on you. But I think I prefer your skin," Thane told her, his mouth scoring down her cheek.

Her hands pressed and probed the strong muscles of his shoulders and back. "I think I like you without clothes too."

Thane moved back from her, his eyes glittering as though her words had pleased him. "Happy to oblige."

"Me too."

In moments they were on the bed, facing each other, passionate and unhidden.

"Shall I tell you something, Thane?"

"Please do."

"I never thought sex could be downright fun, but with you it is."

Thane laughed out loud. "That is the craziest compliment a man could ever get."

"It's true and it *is* a compliment."

The days that followed their marriage were the happiest that Tru had ever known. All the grays in her life seemed to be dissipating in the sunshine Thane brought to her life.

Señor Thane is very good for the little one, señora," Juana told Tru one afternoon when she came to relieve her so that Tru could have lunch with Mel. "I say his name to her and she lights up like the stars."

Tru nodded. "Don't we all?"

Juana chortled. "*Tanto hombría.* Go and eat, Señora Tru."

Tru was laughing at Mel as the baby sat in her play chair gooing at the newest mobile Thane had hung in the huge combination kitchen and family room. The house was beginning to bulge with toys that Thane just "happened" to find.

When the door bell rang, Tru looked around, startled. She wasn't expecting anyone.

"I'll get the door, Juana. Mel is in her play chair," Tru called to the older woman before striding down the long hall that led to the front of the house.

She peered through the glass panels at the side

of the door, but didn't recognize the man. Carefully, she opened the door on the chain.

"Are you Gertrude Wayland?"

"Yes."

"Then this is for you." The man shoved an envelope into her hand, moving back and down one step. "You have been subpoenaed to appear in court. Failure to honor this subpoena can result in a fine, or worse," the man announced before running down the brownstone steps to the street and not looking back.

Paralyzed, Tru's eyes followed him until he turned the corner. All at once her body began to shake. Roger! He'd gone through with his threats!

Tru stared at the paper in her hand as she made her way back to the kitchen, barely noticing Mel. She sat down at the table, sipping her now tepid tea, tasting nothing, pushing aside the uneaten half of her sandwich. The thought of food made her stomach heave.

Pulling herself together at last, she lifted the sleepy baby, took her to her bedroom and put her down for a nap. Then Tru rejoined Juana in the big office behind the kitchen.

"There is nothing special, Señora Tru, but I have a few . . ." Juana's voice trailed away, the messages in her hand forgotten. "What is wrong? Are you ill? Come and sit down. I will get you some hot tea." Juana felt the clamminess of Tru's forehead. "You have been working too hard. You must go to bed. I will handle the messages."

Tru shook her head. "No. I'm not ill, Juana. I'll be fine in a moment. The tea will do the trick." Tru could feel the older woman's worried gaze on her before she shrugged and left the room.

Like a robot, Tru did the work in front of her, answering the phone, taking messages, dealing with the many mini-crises that rose, her voice calm and unemotional while her brain seethed. Mel! God, Roger couldn't take her! Roger was a cold-hearted bastard. He would smother Mel's beautiful personality, destroy her ebullience . . . Her mind went round and round. Time passed, but she wasn't aware of it. At last, she put her head down on her arms, her body quaking with grief at the thought of being without her child.

"Señora Tru, let me help you." Juana put down the teacup, putting her arms around Tru as she sat at the desk, pressing her face to her ample bosom.

"Oh Juana, Juana, I can't lose my child. I can't."

"Señora Tru, do not cry so. No one can take our Mellie from us. Señor Thane would not allow it."

Thane! Tru shivered. Why had she put off telling him about Roger?

"Why don't you lie down for a short time, Señora Tru? I can handle things."

"I'm fine now." Tru gave her a weak smile. "Thank you for the support, dear friend."

Juana walked slowly from the room, but the signs of worry never left her face.

Tru didn't know how long she'd been at the desk, taking messages, fielding questions from prospective customers, when she felt a hand on her shoulder. Her gaze flew to Thane's face. "You're home! What time is it? I didn't realize it was so late."

"It isn't. Juana called me because she was worried about you. She said that you received something in the mail that upset you very much."

"Not in the mail," Tru swallowed painfully, her eyes turning toward the still unopened subpoena.

Thane's gaze followed hers and he picked up the envelope. "This?" At her nod he turned it over in his hand, noting the official letterhead. "You've been subpoenaed."

Tru nodded again, unable to look away from him, but her throat too dry for words.

"I'll get Juana to take over for you and we'll go into the living room."

"The bedroom," Tru managed hoarsely.

Thane frowned at her.

In the bedroom Tru walked to the window like a somnambulist and stared out at the quiet street.

"Are you going to tell me what this is all about, or do you want to me to open it and draw my own conclusions?" Thane said after he closed the bedroom door, noticing how she'd stiffened when he spoke.

"I'll tell you." Tru coughed, but the huskiness didn't leave her voice. "But you might want to read it anyway since I'm not sure where the hearing on whether or not I'm an unfit mother will be."

"What?" Thane muttered.

"Roger is going to try and take Mel away from me."

"From us, don't you mean?" His voice was icy. "Is this what you've been hiding from me?" He saw how Tru's body jerked before curving in an attitude of self defense. "Have you seen him?"

Tru nodded.

"When? Was he here?"

Tru turned away from the window, her face still shadowed, a long sigh escaping her. "Shortly before we married he arrived one day and announced that if I didn't give him the brownstone and maybe the business, he'd sue on the grounds that this was all community property to which he was entitled to half. He . . . he said if I fought he'd prove I was an unfit mother, allowing men to live with me . . ." Tru's voice faded. She watched Thane's hands clench and unclench at his sides, his face working as though he had a mouthful of poison, his eyes mud-colored and dangerous.

"Were you ever going to get around to telling me about this, I mean, if it hadn't come out this way?" He saw her take a step back, but he didn't care. Black fury engulfed him. He had opened himself up to her time and time again, made himself vulnerable, let her know that nothing in his life was hidden from her. But still she had held back from him. "Our marriage seems to be a one-way street, doesn't it?"

"No. I was going to tell you."

"Were you?" Thane flung away from her, yanking off his cashmere suit coat and flinging it against the wall, where it dropped slowly to the floor. Tru stared at the rich material crumpled on the floor.

"Look at me," Thane thundered.

Tru's head swiveled in alarm, her eyes riveted to him. She'd never heard him speak in that threatening tone of voice.

Thane stared back at her, seeing her eyes widen. Blood surged through his veins. His hands and feet tingled and stung as though from frostbite. Not since he'd played professional football had he felt so adrenaline-charged.

"I'll understand if you want to leave . . ." Tru began, then gasped when he made a sudden lunge at her.

"You understand nothing," he bellowed, then held himself in check.

For long moments they stared at each other. Tru was the first to look away.

Thane yanked at his tie, letting it drop to the floor before he ripped open the subpoena and read quickly. Then he went to the phone that sat on the bedside table and punched out some numbers.

"David. Yes, it's Thane. I want to read something to you."

Tru turned back to the window, Thane's words rising and falling behind her like the ebb and flow of the tide. She saw a cardinal land in the denuded maple trees in front of the window; his feathers looked garish against the gray winter day. Suddenly checking the bird feeder seemed a sensible thing to do. Her life might be falling apart, but she could at least make sure the birds had food.

"Where are you going?" Thane had his hand over the mouthpiece of the phone.

"To feed the birds." Tru didn't stop even when she saw his mouth open to call to her.

Eleven

California glistened in the sunlight, momentarily blinding Tru as she accompanied David and Thane out of the courthouse door.

She hadn't uttered a word since the hearing had ended, afraid of setting off Thane's incendiary temper, still shaken by the sight of Roger during the proceedings—he'd looked ready to murder her.

"I'm warning you, Thane. Don't approach him," she'd warned. "If you beat him to a pulp, he'll take you to court again. Isn't it enough that we have Mel?"

Thane had said nothing, only looked at her contemptuously. That had been the way he'd been looking at her ever since the subpoena arrived. Despite his resentment, though, Thane had been quick to set the wheels in motion for the custody hearing. In short order he'd arranged for the two temporaries Tru had hired, to come in full-time to help Juana with the business while they were on the west coast. He had got David Wilson and Billy on the job in California preparing whatever would be needed for Tru's defense.

They had flown out to California two weeks before the hearing so that Tru and David would have time to discuss the many ramifications and intricacies of the case.

Though Tru had been nervous on the day of the hearing, she hadn't been afraid because both Thane and David had been so confident they'd win. They met Roger's charges fully prepared and not only refuted his claims about her unfitness, but also made it plain that Roger Hubbard was guilty of harassment. The judge even issued a restraining order, preventing Roger from ever approaching Mel or her mother again.

"Trying to take our little girl," Thane breathed sulfurously. "I should break his damn neck." Thane stared at Roger as the other man glared back defiantly from the foot of the courthouse steps.

"You think that isn't what he wants?" David admonished his friend sternly. "Your loss of temper could really mess things up." David looked at Tru, thinking she didn't look as spirited as she once had. She had been slender when he'd first met her. Now she was even thinner and her eyes held a pained, frozen expression. "Speak to this husband of yours, will you?"

"There's no need." Thane shrugged. "I'm not going to do anything. Besides, Tru and I have to hurry. We're catching a plane for Hawaii." Tru opened her eyes wide in surprise.

"Good for you. Just what you need. Give my love to that baby of yours. She's a beauty." David kissed Tru good-bye and shook hands with Thane. "My car's around back."

"Shall we go?" Thane took her arm, not waiting for her answer, but steering her toward the Lamborghini that he'd borrowed from his brother-in-law.

On the trip back to the hotel there were no words

between them, but once in their room Tru faced him. "Isn't it a bit silly to go to Maui?"

Mel was spending the day with Thane's sister and her husband.

"I don't think so. Clare and Andrew are dying to take care of Mel, since they're expecting one of their own this year. And we sure as hell have a few things to sort out."

"We can't do it here?"

"Pack your things, Tru. I'll call Linda and my folks."

The flight to Maui was comfortable, long and blessedly uneventful. As the plane circled to land Tru looked out over Diamond Head, unable to stem the emotions that had been building in her since they'd left the mainland.

They were in the Oahu terminal just long enough to receive the traditional leis from Hawaiian dancing girls. Thane guided them to the right gate for the flight to Maui and soon they were aloft again.

He studied her averted profile, her hands threaded together in her lap. "I thought, if you'd like to return to Oahu later for a little sightseeing, we could always take the daily shuttle." His words were courteous, but his voice was hard.

"Thank you." She wanted his forgiveness, his love, not a shopping spree on Oahu. For weeks she had been trying to think of some way to break the ice between then, but words seemed inadequate and there had been Mel to concentrate on. But now there was no reason not to talk. The rift between them was much too wide as it was. But once again they fell silent, and before long it was time to prepare for the descent to Maui.

When Tru saw what Thane and the Sandilins referred to as the "bungalow," she wanted to laugh.

It had four bedrooms and a huge great room. The view from the bay window was like a Gauguin painting. The beach glistened in the sun. The turquoise Pacific seemed too clear to be real.

"Let's swim. It's very warm." Thane turned away, not waiting for her response.

Tru put on a pale blue bikini, noting how her ribs showed though her breasts were as full as ever and her legs looked even longer. She tossed a towel over her shoulder and pushed sand clogs on her feet, then joined Thane on the lanai.

She was too thin. Thane's heart thudded against his ribs as he looked at her. Pain lanced through him as she avoided his eyes. She'd been so unhappy these past weeks . . . and he'd been the principal cause.

"I love you," he told her. "I love you and I've hurt you badly because *I* was hurt. I wanted you to come to me when something was wrong, but you didn't trust me. That hurt, Tru—"

Tru shook her head over and over. "No, no, no. I did trust you. Thane, please, I did." The words came spilling out in her haste to make her point. "I . . . I didn't tell you at first because I was afraid. . . ."

He ground his teeth. "And you agreed to marry me so fast because you figured that I could stand between you and him. Right?"

Tru nodded. "Partly true, but I also loved you. I was a little frightened at how much I could hurt *because* I loved you so much. So much of me belonged to you almost from that first evening when I met you at Ellen's. I loved you then and I do now."

Thane's expression softened, but he didn't touch her.

Tru's hands shot forward in supplication. "After we were married I wanted to forget Roger Hubbard, so I said nothing. I suppose I thought, or hoped, that after a while he'd give up the whole scheme."

"Not that bastard," Thane said through his teeth.

"You're right and I should have known that about him."

"Yes."

Tru stared at him, mute and miserable. There was so much to say to him—that she needed him, that he pulled the sun up for her in the morning and let the moon shine at night. He'd filled her with exuberance, laughter, and joy. Without him life would be a desert, tinged with gray.

"Your smile is lopsided," Thane told her solemnly.

"That's because I haven't had much practice smiling lately. What did you say about swimming?"

Thane tipped his head to one side as a gesture for her to precede him. As she did so, he noted every quiver of the body in front of him, the fluidity of motion, the inborn grace that set his blood racing.

Tru flung herself into the surf, striking out strongly, Thane at her side. When she knew that they were out in deep water, much higher than their heads, she turned to him, sweeping her salty blond strands back from her face, treading water easily.

"I didn't have the strength to walk to you on land. I needed the ocean to make me lighter." She flung herself at him, clutching him, making them both submerge. Tru wanted him in that moment more than she'd ever wanted him before.

Thane put his mouth over hers, breathing air into her before he brought her to the surface. "Is something wrong? Are you cramped?"

"No," Tru responded serenely. "I wanted you to know what I wasn't able to say back there on the beach . . . that win, lose, or draw, I'm yours, whether you keep me or throw me away, it won't matter. If we live a continent apart or in the same room, my fate is joined with yours. And what I feel for you won't fade away in this lifetime or any other."

"And my destiny is locked with yours." Thane held her easily, his face relaxing, his eyes heating.

"I thought I'd lost you," Tru whimpered, not trying to stem the tears that gathered at her eyes.

"You couldn't. I belonged to you before the world began."

"That's a long time," Tru responded shakily, smiling through her tears.

"And I'll be yours when we have been in our graves a thousand years."

Tru nodded and leaned forward to put her mouth on his. Then she looked around, startled. "We've drifted out too far."

Thane shook his head. "Nothing is going to happen to us. I won't let it."

They swam for shore side by side, sure and complete.

"I hope you feel like making love," Tru told him, coming out of the ocean, glancing at him sideways as the water combed back from her legs, a little out of breath from her exertions. "I'm in the mood to make another baby."

"We didn't make Mel, darling," Thane said, as he swept her up into his arms.

Tru looked surprised. "That's right. We didn't. I forgot." She threw her arms around his neck and laughed out loud with the sheer joy of living.

"I'm sure you won't forget making baby number two, love."

"No, Thane, my darling, I don't think I will. I love you so very much and I want to . . ." she whispered to him.

Tru laughed when Thane started to run toward the bungalow, holding her tight in his arms.

THE EDITOR'S CORNER

Thanks for all your wonderful cards and letters telling us how glad you are that we've added two LOVESWEPTS to our monthly publishing list. Obviously, it's quite a lot of additional work, and, so, we are especially glad to welcome Kate Hartson as our new senior editor. Kate has been in publishing for more than seven years and has edited many different kinds of works, but in the last few years she has devoted a great deal of her time to romance fiction and has edited almost one hundred love stories. Kate is as fine a person as she is an editor, and we are delighted to have her on our team.

You have six delicious treats to anticipate next month from Peggy Webb, Sandra Brown, Joan Elliott Pickart, Kay Hooper, Charlotte Hughes, and Iris Johansen. I probably don't need to say more than those six names to make you eager to get at the books—but I had so much fun working on them that it would be virtually impossible for me to restrain myself from sharing my enthusiasm with you.

Peggy Webb presents a heartrending love story in **PRIVATE LIVES**, LOVESWEPT #216. John Riley is a man whose brilliant singing career has left him somewhat burned out; Sam Jones is an enchanting woman who blunders into his rural retreat and brings more sunshine and fresh tickling breezes into his life than he could get in the great outdoors. This moving romance is a bit of a departure into more serious emotional writing for Peggy, though she doesn't leave her characteristic humor behind. Her lovers are wonderful, and we think their healing power on each other will leave you feeling marvelous long after you've finished reading about their **PRIVATE LIVES**.

FANTA C, Sandra Brown's LOVESWEPT #217, is a sheer delight. On the surface heroine Elizabeth Burke seems to be a bit straitlaced, but her occupation—and her daydreams—reveal her to be a sensual and romantic lady. She owns and operates a boutique in a large hotel called Fantasy, where she sells such items as silk lingerie and seductive perfumes. It is in her rich and powerful fantasy life that she expresses her real self . . . until neighbor Thad Randolph comes to her rescue, dares to fulfill her secret dreams, and turns fantasy into reality. A keeper, if there ever was one!

LUCKY PENNY by Joan Elliott Pickart is LOVESWEPT #218 and another real winner from this talented and prolific author. Penelope Chapman is a complicated woman with a wealth of passion and sweet sympathy beneath her successful exterior. Cabe Malone is a man who secretly yearns for a woman to cherish and build a life with. They meet when Cabe finds her weeping in the house he is building . . . and his very protective instinct is aroused. Soon, though, Penny must flee, and Cabe sets off in hot pursuit. A breathlessly exciting chase ensues, and you'll cheer when these two lovable people capture each other.

News Flash! Kay Hooper is being held hostage by a band of

(continued)

dangerous, sexy men, and they aren't going to let her go until she's finished telling the love story of each and every one of them. And aren't we lucky? Fasten your seatbelts, because with **RAFFERTY'S WIFE**, LOVESWEPT #219, Kay is going to sweep you away on another glorious caper. This time that sneaky Hagen has Rafferty Lewis and Sarah Cavell in his clutches. He's assigned them the roles of husband and wife on an undercover assignment that takes them to an island paradise in the midst of revolution. But Rafferty and Sarah are falling deeply, hopelessly in love, and their madness for each other is almost as desperate as the job they have to do. Watch out for Sereno . . . and don't think that just because Raven and Josh are on their honeymoon they are going to be out of the romantic action. It's only fair to tell you that Kay has created a marvelous series for you. Look next for **ZACH's LAW**, then **THE FALL OF LUCAS KENDRICK,** then . . . well, more on this from me next month!

Exciting, evocative, and *really original* aptly describe, LOVESWEPT #220, **STRAIGHT SHOOTIN' LADY** by Charlotte Hughes. When Maribeth Bradford comes to the bank in her small town to interview with its handsome new president for a job, she walks into a robbery in progress. Suddenly, she finds herself bound back-to-back with devastatingly attractive Edward Spears and locked with him in a dark closet. . . . And that's just the beginning of a great love story between a devoted small-town gal and a city slicker with a lot of adjustments to make. We think you're going to be utterly charmed by this wonderful romance.

THE SPELLBINDER, LOVESWEPT #221, by Iris Johansen delivers precisely what the title promises—a true spellbinder of a love story. Brody Devlin can hypnotize an audience as easily as he can overwhelm a woman with his virile good looks. Sacha Lorion is a waif with wild gypsy beauty who has a claim on Brody. Her past is dark, mysterious, dangerous . . . and when her life is threatened, Brody vows to protect her. Both of them swiftly learn that they must belong to one another body and soul . . . 'til death do them part. This is a magnificent story full of force and fire.

Enjoy!

Sincerely,

Carolyn Nichols

Carolyn Nichols
   Editor

LOVESWEPT
Bantam Books, Inc.
666 Fifth Avenue
New York, NY 10103

Imagine yourself Loveswept®

SHEER MADNESS

SHEER BRILLIANCE

SHEER ROMANCE

SHEER PASSION

SHEER COLOR

All it takes is a little imagination and more Pazazz.

CLAIROL
PAZAZZ®
SHEER COLOR WASH

PAZAZZ SHEER COLOR WASH: 8 inspiring sheer washes of color that wash out in four shampoos.

PAZAZZ SHEER COLOR WASH:
TRY THEM ALL AND BE LOVESWEPT.
Look for Pazazz Sheer Color Wash in the haircolor section.

HANDSOME, SPACE-SAVER
BOOKRACK

Ilevco US Pat. 3,464,565

ONLY
$9.95

- hand-rubbed walnut finish
- patented sturdy construction
- assembles in seconds
- assembled size 16" x 8"

Perfect as a desk or table top library— Holds both hardcovers and paperbacks.

 **LOVESWEPT**

Love Stories you'll never forget by authors you'll always remember

☐	21795	**Where The Heart Is #174** Eugenia Riley	$2.50
☐	21796	**Expose #175** Kimberli Wagner	$2.50
☐	21794	**'Til The End Of Time #176** Iris Johansen	$2.50
☐	21802	**Hard Habit To Break #177** Linda Cajio	$2.50
☐	21807	**Disturbing The Peace #178** Peggy Webb	$2.50
☐	21801	**Kaleidoscope #179** Joan Elliott Pickart	$2.50
☐	21797	**The Dragon Slayer #180** Patt Bucheister	$2.50
☐	21790	**Robin And Her Merry People #181** Fayrene Preston	$2.50
☐	21756	**Makin' Whoopee #182** Billie Green	$2.50
☐	21811	**Tangles #183** Barbara Boswell	$2.50
☐	21812	**Sultry Nights #184** Anne Kolaczyk & Ed Kolaczyk	$2.50
☐	21809	**Sunny Chandler's Return #185**	$2.50
☐	21810	**Fiddlin' Fool #186** Susan Richardson	$2.50
☐	21814	**Last Bridge Home #187** Iris Johansen	$2.50
☐	21822	**Detour To Euphoria #188** Becky Lee Weyrich	$2.50
☐	21798	**In Serena's Web #189** Kay Hooper	$2.50
☐	21823	**Wild Poppies #190** Joan Elliott Pickart	$2.50
☐	21828	**Across the River of Yesterday #191** Iris Johansen	$2.50
☐	21813	**The Joy Bus #192** Peggy Webb	$2.50
☐	21824	**Raven On the Wing #193** Kay Hooper	$2.50
☐	21829	**Not A Marrying Man #194** Barbara Boswell	$2.50
☐	21825	**Wind Warning #195** Sara Orwig	$2.50
☐	21771	**Solid Gold Prospect #196** Hertha Schulze	$2.50

Special Offer
Buy a Bantam Book
for only 50¢.

Now you can have Bantam's catalog filled with hundreds of titles plus take advantage of our unique and exciting bonus book offer. A special offer which gives you the opportunity to purchase a Bantam book for only 50¢. Here's how!

By ordering any five books at the regular price per order, you can also choose any other single book listed (up to a $5.95 value) for just 50¢. Some restrictions do apply, but for further details why not send for Bantam's catalog of titles today!

Just send us your name and address and we will send you a catalog!